PUFFIN BOOKS

the Ribbajack
& Other Curious Yarns

Actor, playwright and BBC presenter, Brian Jacques is also a fearsome storyteller, singer, sailor and all-round scallywag! He is the world-renowned author of the best-selling Redwall series and many other popular books for children of all ages. Before he began writing, his life was as full of adventure as the stories he creates – at the age of fifteen he went to sea and travelled the world, before returning to his home town of Liverpool, where he still lives.

BRIAN JACQUES

the Ribbajack

& Other Curious Yarns

PUFFIN

Penguin G   (USA) Inc.   , New York   10014, USA
Penguin Group (, Canada M4P 2Y3

Penguin Irelan   nguin Books Ltd)
Penguin Grou (Australia),   3124, Australia

Penguin Books In   Pvt Ltd, 11 C   lhi – 110 017, India
Penguin Group (310, New Zealand

Penguin Books (South Africa) (Pty) Ltd, 24 Sturdee Avenue, Rosebank, Johannesburg 2196,
South Africa

Penguin Books Ltd, Registered Offices: 80 Strand, London WC2R 0RL, England

penguin.com

First published in the USA by Philomel Books,
a division of Penguin Group (USA), Inc, 2004
First published in Great Britain in Puffin Books 2006
1

Text copyright © by Redwall La Dita Ltd, 2004
All rights reserved

The moral right of the author has been asserted

Set in Trump Mediaeval
Made and printed in England by Clays Ltd, St Ives plc

British Library Cataloguing in Publication Data

A CIP catalogue record for this book is
available from the British Library

ISBN-13: 978–0–141–32166–0
ISBN-10: 0–141–32166–0

To my sons, Marc and David

Contents

the Ribbajack

GENTLE READER, HEED MY PLEA,
pray witness now this shocking tale,
'twas told to me by one, forsooth,
who vowed he spoke the honest truth,
he took an oath, he told no lies,
and swore it on his own three eyes!

End of Term, Summer 1937

Archibald Smifft was worse than any plague or pestilence known to man. This was the unanimous consensus of opinion by all at the boarding school of Duke Crostacious the Inviolate. Teachers, pupils, groundsmen, cooks and all ancillary staff were in total agreement on this, and who, pray, would deny their assessment?

A single glance at the boy in question would confirm the fears of even a stranger. Archibald Smifft was indeed the raw material from which nightmares were made. From the top of his scrofulous bullet-shaped head, with its jug-handle ears and ski-jump nose, the beady eyes (which had often been compared to those of an ill-tempered cobra) glaring out from the spotted moon crater of a face, right down from his rounded shoulders, pot belly and wart-scarred knees, to the fallen arches of his flat feet, the Smifft boy was the very portrait of villainy, viciousness and malicious intent.

He had been abandoned as a baby on the school driveway, sitting smugly in an outrageously expensive bassinet. In one hand the child clutched a chamois bag containing a king's ransom in uncut rubies; in the other, a recently dead frog. Attached to his satin pillow was a note: "Deer sur. Pleez giv Archibald a gud ejercayshun an bring him up propper. Maw roobeez to folloh. Singed, X Smifft. Pee yess. He lykes byting thingz."

The headmaster, a gentle, trusting man named Aubrey Plother, I.O.U.E. (Institute of Unskilled Educators), and the matron, Mrs. Twogg, were the two who found the infant. Trying hard to avoid Archibald's malevolent smirk, Mr. Plother's heart softened. He snatched the bag of rubies, declaring charitably, "Mrs. Twogg, marm, I feel we would be neglecting our Christian duty were we not to adopt and care for this unfortunate waif. I have decided he shall receive the benefits of a thorough education here at my establishment!"

The matron, who had left her glasses indoors and would never admit she had dreadful eyesight, swept the babe up in her huge pink arms. She tickled its bottom lip fondly. "Oh, bless you for the kindly soul you are, Headmaster. Poor little mite, shame on the one who abandoned you. Coochy-cooch, my little cherub!"

The infant left off chewing his frog long enough to inflict a bite on Mrs. Twogg's index finger that a tiger shark would have envied. The matron wore her glasses at all times after that afternoon so that she would be able to immediately decipher further communications left on the pillows of abandoned children. That is how Archibald Smifft came to be inflicted on his present school.

For my more gentle and nervous readers, I will draw a veil over the intervening eleven years. Except to mention, in passing, four teachers' resignations (diagnosed as mentally traumatised), an explosion in the pupils' chemistry laboratory, the disappearance of four cats belonging to the gardener's wife, several major floods in the washrooms, a fire which destroyed the sports pavilion and a school mastiff that vanished without trace. These, and a host of other indignities, atrocities and miscellaneous mishaps—students absconding to foreign territories, etc.—were all in one way or another attributable to said Archibald Smifft. However, the headmaster's kind heart, plus the prompt arrival each term of a bag containing rubies by special delivery to Aubrey Plother, I.O.U.E., insured the boy's continuance at Crostacious the Inviolate Boarding School for young gentlemen. Granted, there were frequent staff walkouts, but the headmaster furthered his name as a good man by rewarding injured, faithful and long-serving staff members by giving them a ruby apiece as an annual incentive.

Archibald's dormitory was a long, draughty room. It contained only two boys besides himself. Wilton Minor and Peterkin Soames were far too frightened to cut and run like the others—they lived in constant terror of their small but vengeful roommate. Together each night, the wretched pair huddled on their beds at the room's far end, constantly casting fearful glances at Archibald's den. This was a high screen of assorted rubbish which he had coerced them into building at the other end of the dormitory. Wilton and Soames both had families posted overseas in the military and colonial services. As a result, they were permanent boarders, spending all holidays, vacations and non-term times on the school premises, with Archibald Smifft for company. He delighted in terrorising the hapless duo, each day bringing fresh horrors for Wilton and Soames. Wilton Minor, the more delicate of the two, had found grey hairs whilst parting his hair on his eleventh birthday! Both boys had a wan-faced, hunted look about them.

One day close to the summer term break, all the pupils were taken on an educational trip to a local dairy farm. Everybody, even Archibald, was required to go. This provided the headmaster and matron with a golden opportunity to inspect the Smifft dormitory. They were forced into this task frequently. The area occupied by Archibald was a place where any intruder had to tread with extreme caution. It was a task which Mr. Plother and Mrs. Twogg did not relish. However, if the dormitory where the Smifft boy laid his scheming little head to rest each night went unchecked, the possible consequences could prove both horrendous and dire.

Filled with trepidation, the pair made their way upstairs. The headmaster was armed with a pair of fireside tongs, some stout leathern gauntlets and a golf club. Mrs. Twogg carried a furled umbrella, a bottle of strong disinfectant, a sharp knitting needle and a flashlight.

A notice was posted on the dormitory door, pinned to the tail of a rat skeleton.

KEEYP OWT WEN A. SMIFFT IZ NOT HEER. YOO HAV BEAN WORNED!

Being a more regular visitor to boys' dormitories than her superior, the matron placed herself in front, reassuring him, "Stand back, Headmaster, I'll deal with this!"

Keeping her distance, the intrepid lady took a fencing stance, then lunged, giving the door a sharp push with her brolly tip. The customary avalanche of flour, soot, glue and sour milk thundered down as the booby-trapped door swung inward.

The headmaster's knuckles whitened as he gripped his golf club. "Capital work, Matron, you're an absolute brick!"

He ventured forward, but Mrs. Twogg thrust him aside with a cry. "Wait!" With a neat twist of her knitting needle, she snapped the almost invisible length of black cotton which was stretched across the threshold.

Zzzzzip thunk!

A lethal-looking spear stood quivering in the door-post at neck height. She studied it and identified the weapon.

"Hmm, Jivaro headhunting spear, probably tipped with some kind of poison. Curare, I suspect. Don't touch it, Headmaster."

Shaking his head, Aubrey Plother entered the room. "That's odd. Smifft got an F minus in geography and chemistry last term."

Mrs. Twogg gave the headmaster another shove, which sent him skittering in a semicircle. "Don't step on that floorboard—as I recall, that's the one with the steel-jawed foxtrap beneath it!"

Mr. Plother stepped gingerly around the offending timber. "A revelation indeed, Matron. Smifft showed no interest in either carpentry or nature study. Hmm, resourceful boy, eh?"

Mrs. Twogg narrowed her eyes. "Right, let's see what holds the little villain's attention these days, Headmaster."

Their search brought forward the usual stuff. Some detonators, various stink bombs, a complete flea circus and an inflatable rubber cushion capable of producing a variety of extremely rude noises. Mrs. Twogg surveyed the haul. "Nothing of any great note here. Anything under there, Headmaster?"

Mr. Plother, who had been exploring underneath Archibald's bed, scrambled out backwards on all fours, red-faced and excited. "Help me to move this bed out from the wall, Matron, there's a lot of stuff hidden beneath it."

He jumped aside as the matron moved the bed with a single heave. They stared in horror at the collection of books, jars and apparatus which lay uncovered. Mr. Plother gasped.

"Sorcery, necromancy, wizardry! Oh, deary me!"

The worthy matron shone her torch over the unsavoury heap. "We were fortunate to have found this in time, sir. Look at the labels on these jars. Eye of Lizard, Skin of Worm, Tooth of Rat, Limb of Toad! Oh, the vile boy!"

Craning her head sideways, she read the titles of the books which were strewn about the floor.

"*The Secrets of Medieval Warlocks. Voodoo in Six Easy Steps. You Too Can Conjure Up the Spirits. Tortures of the Spanish Inquisition. How to Become a Master of Malice.* This is a library of the dark arts, how did Smifft get it all?"

Mr. Plother was studying a deck of tarot cards and a Ouija board. He dusted absently at his gown. "Well, at least he's reading. Hello, what's this?"

The matron swept a shrunken head from his hand. "Don't you realise the danger this school is in, Headmaster? Archibald Smifft is learning the forbidden arts, black magic!"

Aubrey Plother blinked nervously over the rim of his glasses. "Oh, good grief, you're right, marm. What do you suggest we do?"

A shrill, harsh voice interrupted them. "I suggest you leave my stuff alone, and get out of my room, right now!" Archibald Smifft stood framed in the doorway, his beady eyes flickering angrily from one to the other as he hissed, "Go on, clear out, or you'll both be sorry!"

The headmaster wilted under the fiendish glare. He dithered, "Ah, yes, er, Smifft. Back from the dairy farm early, aren't we?"

Archibald strode forward and tugged his bed back into place. "The others are still there, I wasn't allowed to stay. Huh, just because all the milk turned sour and a big cheese fell on the farmer's wife. Just as well I came right back, eh? What do you two think you're doing in my dorm? Speak up!"

Mrs. Twogg pushed the headmaster behind her. Puffing up to her full matronly height, she glared down at the boy. "Archibald Smifft, how dare you take that tone to your elders and betters! Explain yourself, what is the meaning of all that dreadful rubbish beneath your bed?"

Archibald's eyes narrowed to slits. He pointed a grubby finger at the matron and made a brief incantantion:

> "By the lifeless eye from a dead man's socket,
> see what lies within thy pocket."

One thing Mrs. Twogg could not abide was a cockroach. Placing her hand in her overall pocket, she encountered not one, but four of the large, fat insects writhing about there. She fled the dormitory, gurgling loudly in disgust.

Mr. Plother was still dithering indecisively as Archibald turned the grimy finger upon him, chanting:

> *"Flies which feed from long-dead flesh,*
> *growing fat on some cold face,*
> *soon will circle round your head,*
> *if you do not leave this place!"*

The headmaster uttered one loud word (well, three, if you count *Yee harr wooh* separately). Archibald sat upon his bed, listening to the unfortunate man taking the stairs two at a time as he beat furiously at the cloud of big bluebottles which were attacking his head. Reaching beneath the bed, Archibald drew forth his favourite book. For over an hour, he leafed through the volume of spells and curses, muttering darkly in frustration.

"Hmph, flies, spiders, wasps and worms, beginners' stuff! I need something better. Bigger, more powerful, something really bad and terrifying. A monster, that's what I need!"

Soames and Wilton had entered the dormitory via the door at the far end, since they were not allowed to use Archibald's door. As quietly as possible, both boys took out their P.E. kit. They could hear Archibald ranting on from behind his barricade.

"*Voodoo in Six Easy Steps*—what good is that to

me? There's not a spleen of python or a tooth of croc-odile for miles around, or a sting of scorpion!"

Wilton's bedside locker door creaked as he tried to open it silently. He winced as Archibald's unsightly head popped up over the top of the barricade.

"Where do you two think you're going?"

Soames gulped visibly. "Oh, er, hello there, Smifft. We were just getting changed for P.E. in the gym. Aren't you coming?"

Archibald sneered. "Nah, no time for that rubbish. Anyhow, old Bamford won't be there, he's got a swollen foot. Horsefly bite, I think."

Wilton thrust one foot into a shoe. "But we just saw him when we came back from the dairy farm visit. Mr. Bamford looked alright then. He told us to get changed into P.E. kit, said he wanted to see you in the gym, too."

Archibald glanced at the wall clock. "Oh, it's only two-fifteen. Don't worry, by half past, old Bamford should have a swollen foot, trust me."

Just then, Bertie Rivington from the next dorm shoved his head around the doorway. "I say, you chaps heard the latest? P.E. cancelled. Old Bammers was stung by some whopping great wasp. His foot's swollen up like a balloon, all red and puffy!"

As Rivington ran off to spread the news, Archibald shrugged. "See, I told you. Huh, that idiot Rivington doesn't know the difference between a wasp and a horsefly. Anyhow, you two aren't going anywhere. Sit down, I want a word with you both. Sit down, I said, the sound of your knees knocking is beginning to annoy me."

Soames and Wilton obeyed with alacrity. It did not pay to annoy Archibald Smifft.

The headmaster sneezed vigorously, his hair still damp from Zappit, the lilac-scented fly spray. As he wiped his eyes on a fresh kerchief, a knock sounded on his study door. He sneezed as he called out, "Entaaachah!"

"Gesundheit, Headmaster!"

Mrs. Twogg entered, clad in a crisply starched and laundered uniform. She sat down, shuddering slightly at the memory of cockroaches roaming around in her pocket. "Headmaster, something must be done about the Smifft boy! These dreadful things he is practising will bring the school to rack and ruin. I insist that you act immediately!"

Mr. Plother stifled another sneeze, looking blankly at her. "Smifft, ah, yes. Er, what do you suggest we do, Matron?"

She consulted her fob watch. It was shortly before three. "Invite the school chaplain to tea, we must seek his advice. Men of the cloth usually know about exorcising demons and countering the forbidden arts."

Mr. Plother picked up the phone and began dialling. "It's worth a try, I suppose, but the Padre may be a bit out of his depth with occult matters."

Archibald perched cross-legged on the bed. From under beetling brows he scanned his quaking dormitory companions. They waited on his words with bated breath. "Listen, you two, I need a monster, a really scary one. So, have you got any ideas?"

Wilton stammered, "A m-monster, wh-what d'you m-mean?"

Their interrogator gnawed thoughtfully on a dirt-encrusted fingernail. "I'm not quite sure exactly. Put it this way, Wilty. What could frighten the daylights out of you, eh?"

Wilton's answer was not overly helpful. "Y-you, S-Smifft."

The malevolent stare turned to Soames. "What about you?"

A nervous tic began afflicting the boy's right eye. "Er, you, I suppose."

Their tormentor bounded from the bed, causing both boys to jump with fright as he exploded at them. "You suppose? Listen, you two dithering dummies, you'd better start coming up with some proper answers. You know what happened to Bamford. I can conjure up bees and wasps, you know. Ones that can give nasty stings to a chap's rear end. Then chaps have to drop their pants so Matron can treat them. So you'd better talk fast, understand?"

Tears beaded in Wilton's eyes. His lip began quivering. "Wh-what d-d'you want us to say, S-Smifft?"

Archibald pounded the bedside locker top. "Don't you dare start blubbering, Wilton, just answer my question. What really terrifies you, eh? A bogeyman, a vampire, a ghost, a spook! What? Tell me!"

Wilton practically yelped his answer. "The dark! I've always been frightened of the dark."

Archibald nodded. "So that's why you're always lurking under the sheets with your torch on after lights out. Huh, you'd better come up with something good, Soames."

Peterkin Soames blinked hard, pausing awhile before he spoke. "The only think I can think of is the Ribbajack."

Smifft's mad eyes lit up hopefully. "What's the Ribbajack? Tell me all about it. Now!"

Soames tried to avoid Archibald's maniacal stare. He told what little he knew about the oddly named Ribbajack. "My father is with the B.O.C.S., that's the British Overseas Colonial Services. Actually, he's an assistant district commissioner in Burma, stationed in an area called the Paktai Hills. He says it's a rather strange country, with lots of beliefs and superstitions which we know very little about."

Archibald interrupted abruptly. "What about this Ribbajack?"

Soames flinched under the savage intensity of the question. "Actually, I have one of Daddy's letters from last term. It mentions the Ribbajack. Would you like to see it, Smifft?"

Archibald was in a frenzy of anticipation. "Yes, yes, get it!"

Grabbing the large manila envelope from Soames, he pulled from it several vellum sheets of B.O.C.S. crested writing paper. There was also a photograph of a British couple and an elderly Burmese gentleman standing on the verandah of a large, elegant bungalow. It had writing on the back: *Yrs truly, the memsahib, and Ghural Panjit, my interpreter. Chindwin 1935.*

Archibald gave the letter to Soames. "Read it out loud." Soames steadied his voice and read the text.

> My dearest Peterkin,
> How are you, old chap, doing rather well at school, I hope. Mother sends her love. Sorry we cannot make it home for the hols. But chin up and keep smiling, otherwise I'll send the Ribbajack to sort you out (ha ha, only joking of course). Bet you've never heard of a Ribbajack. Young chaps like you would be jolly interested in it. Let me explain.
> The locals out here blame all misfortunes and deaths to it. Missing persons, and so on, it's always the

Ribbajack. I first heard of it when my interpreter, a splendid fellow named Ghural, accompanied me to settle a dispute. We travelled to a village high in the hills where it seemed a man had gone missing. Of course, everyone said it was due to the Ribbajack.

Apparently, the local carpenter had promised his daughter in marriage to a herdsman. The dispute arose when this herdsman accused the carpenter of cheating him on the dowry price of the girl, a common enough occurrence out here. Well, pretty soon after, the carpenter went missing without trace. Quite frankly, it was my considered opinion that the herdsman had killed the carpenter and done away with the body. He was a proud man, you see, and could not be seen as a laughingstock by the villagers. Ghural, and all the locals, insisted that the carpenter had been taken by a Ribbajack, so there was no point in searching for him. I was surprised at Ghural, as he is a well-educated man. It took some persuading to get him to tell me about the Ribbajack, but here's what he said.

"Sir, if a man believes in the Ribbajack, then he can create one in his own mind, and it will come alive. If a man has a hated enemy whom he wants to be rid of, here is what he does. He makes a picture in his imagination of a monster. It is the most horrible creature he can think of, with the body of a crocodile, three eyes, long poison teeth, and other such dreadful features. The harder he concentrates, the more real his Ribbajack becomes. Then, in the darkness, one midnight hour, the creature will appear to him, as solid as you or I, sir.

"It will speak to him thus. . . .

*'From the pits of darkness in your
    mind,*
*I am Ribbajack, born out of human
    spite.*
*Say the name of the one I am brought
    to find,*
*command me to take him forever
    from sight.'*

"From that night on, sir, the Ribbajack is never again seen, and neither is your enemy. I have heard tales, some of Ribbajacks who turned on their creators because they could not take the one whom the creator named. A Ribbajack never takes more than one victim. It is the fate of the Ribbajack, and the one it takes, to disappear from the world of men."

Pretty scary stuff, eh, Peterkin? But your dad wasn't about to believe all that mumbo-jumbo, and neither should you, old chap. Tell you what I did. I had the herdsman clapped in prison for five years. Then I confiscated all his cattle and had them paid to the carpenter's family as compensation. That's British justice for you, tempered by the local traditions, of course.

But enough of Jibbaracks, old fellow. Keep your shoulder to the wheel, and your nose to the grindstone. Make your mother and me proud of you when next we meet. Though the way things are out here, heaven knows when that will be. Ours not to reason why, etc.

Keep smiling. Toodle pip and all that.

Yr Pater.

When Soames finished reading, Archibald snatched the letter and pocketed it, snarling, "Got any more stuff about the Ribbajack?"

Soames shook his head. "Nothing, I'm afraid, it was

only mentioned in that one letter. I say, Smifft, can I have my letter back? I keep everything my parents write. Though it's not very much, they're always very busy, you see."

Archibald Smifft snarled at him, "No, you can't, I want to read it again for myself. I've got work to do now, so beat it, you two."

Wilton and Soames fled the dormitory, relieved that their ordeal was over. Soames felt lucky to have got away with just the loss of a letter, Wilton ruing the fact that he had revealed his fear of the dark. As they emerged onto the driveway, he whispered to his pal, "I say, Peterkin, it looks like Smifft is cooking something pretty horrible up, what d'you think?"

Soames thrust both hands into his blazer pockets. "Rather, he's up to some wickedness, I'm sure. I don't like it one little bit. One thing's certain, though, we can't be left alone in that dorm with Smifft for almost two months' summer hols. How much money have you got, chum?"

Wilton frowned. "In my money box there's two fivers from my parents last Christmas. What do we need money for?"

Soames did some quick calculating. "I've got six pounds from my people last birthday, and a ten-bob note left from my allowance. What d'you say we go and stay at my aunt Adelaide's place for the recess? It's up in Yorkshire, at Harrogate. Come on, let's take a walk down to the post office, I'll give her a ring." He broke into a trot. Wilton ran to keep up with him.

"What about me, d'you think she'll mind terribly?"

His friend chuckled. "What, Aunt Addie? Not a bit, old man. She's half deaf and totally nutty. Lives alone, except for a cook and gardener, in a great rambling place up by the moors. She's got loads of cats, and keeps geese, too. We'll be safe from Smifft up there for the summer. Are you game?"

Wilton felt as though a great weight had been lifted from his young heart. "Rather! Lead on, old chap, I'd sooner be marooned on the ocean in a bathtub than be stuck with that bounder Smifft for the hols!"

Less than an hour later, both boys skipped blithely out of the telephone box. Soames rubbed his hands together joyfully.

"Here we are, all set to go. There's a train for Harrogate at seven-ten this evening, should get us in about ten. Aunt Addie is sending old Jenkins the gardener to pick us up in the car. All we've got to do is pack a case each. The dreaded Smifft shouldn't even notice we're gone, you know how he is when he's swotting up a foul new scheme. Come on, race you back!"

The school chaplain of Duke Crostacious the Inviolate was Reverend Rodney Miller, a bluff, hearty old fel-

low. He was known by several nicknames: the Sky
Pilot, Big Dusty, Rev, or the Padre. This was owing to
his long service with the King's Lancashire Rifle Reg-
iment. He had spent many years in India, Burma and
Bhutan as Padre to the soldiers. Rev. Miller stood well
over six feet tall, a portly, congenial figure with a fiery
complexion and white bushy eyebrows. He had an ex-
tensive fund of stories about life in the far-flung out-
posts of empire—it had been said that he could bore
the legs off a table with them.

Rev. Miller sat in the headmaster's study, taking
tea with Mrs. Twogg and Mr. Plother. Helping himself
to slices of Dundee cake and Bath Oliver biscuits,
washed down with copius amounts of Darjeeling tea,
he listened to them holding forth on the subject of
Archibald Smifft—the boy's unhealthy fascination
with occult magic and the forbidden arts. The matron
explained about the materials they had discovered beneath the bed and the possible atrocities Smifft could
wreak upon both them and the school. The headmaster recounted the incident of the cockroaches and flies.
Rev. Miller sucked the chocolate from a Bath Oliver,
and dunked it in his tea reflectively.

"Ah, yes, the old jiggery pokery, y'know. Saw quite
a bit of it for m'self out on the subcontinent, India and
all that. By Jove, watched a chap climb up a rope and
vanish into thin air. Amazing! Where the dickens he
went to, I'll never know. Another time I saw a fakir

take a pair of live scorpions—d'you know what he did with 'em, eh?"

The matron poured more tea, remarking primly, "I'm sure we'd shudder to think, Reverend. However, this isn't getting us anywhere with the Smifft problem, don't you agree, Headmaster?"

Mr. Plother blinked over the rim of his Crown Derby teacup. "Er, precisely, Mrs. Twogg, the boy is definitely involved in some murky matters. I mean, how d'you explain a cloud of flies swarming around my head, Padre?"

The chaplain picked a few crumbs from his ample stomach. "Huh, flies, y'say, I could do that. Slap a dab of honey on my head. Flies'd flock to it. A few wasps and a bee or two, as well, I should imagine, eh?"

The matron pursed her lips. "Really, Reverend, I don't consider this a fit subject for humour. You have been invited here to give assistance in what we think is a serious matter!"

Rev. Miller heaved himself out of the creaking armchair. He sighed regretfully at the empty cake stand. "Right you are, marm, suppose I'd better go and have a few words with the young scamp. What's the chap's name, Smithers?"

Mrs. Twogg's chins wobbled as she snapped out the name. "Smifft. Archibald Smifft. You remember him from Christmas term, surely!"

The chaplain's bushy eyebrows rose. "Good Lord,

that fellow? Wasn't he the rogue who sabotaged my
incense burner with stink bombs at the chapel service? Short, grubby cove, with his eyes too close together? Never liked boys with close-together eyes,
y'know. Reminds me of a gunnery corporal I served
with at Hyderabad, furtive little blighter. Caught him
one time in the officers' mess, had half a bottle of
Madeira and some vindaloo curry powder. You'll never
guess what the scallywag was up to—"

The matron interrupted him abruptly. "Smifft!"

Rev. Miller recalled his errand. "Eh, what? Oh, yes,
I'll go and have a talk with Master Smithers. No time
like the present!"

Archibald Smifft lay flat on his bed, exerting all his
mental powers to produce an image of how a Ribbajack might look. He ignored the muffled rummaging
of Wilton and Soames on the other side of his barricade, for they could be dealt with later. His Ribbajack
was all-important. The description penned by
Soames's father sounded fairly good. But Archibald
had decided it needed some adjustments to suit his
macabre taste. A crocodile's body, he would keep that
feature. Three eyes? No, his would have just one big
eye, a disgusting red runny one. Then there was the
question of the arms. What if they were long, right
down to its feet, hairy like a gorilla's, and studded
with suckers, similar to an octopus's tentacles? The

long, sharp teeth sounded a bit humdrum. Suppose it had a feathered head and a great hooked parrot beak, which could rip and tear and chop? Perfect! It would be his own personal and original Ribbajack.

Archibald's train of thought was broken by someone knocking on the door outside his den. He attempted to dismiss it at this crucial stage of his image-making. However, it was not about to cease, in fact the knocking doubled in volume and insistence, then a voice.

"Come on, young man, I know you're in there. Met two of your pals on the corridor below on their way out, they told me. Listen, Smithers, if you don't open this door pretty sharply, I'll bring my old service pistol and blow the lock off. D'you hear me, Smithers?"

Rev. Miller put his ear to the door just as it opened. He practically fell in on top of a scowling, ill-tempered boy. (This would have solved the problem neatly, as the Rev. weighed in at somewhere around two and a half hundred pounds. What a lark! Man of the cloth flattens young schoolboy by accident.) Smiling at the thought, the chaplain took the jovial approach. He winked companionably at the irate boy. "What ho, young Smithers, come to have a friendly word with you. At the headmaster's and matron's request, of course. Well, aren't you going to ask the old Sky Pilot in, eh?"

Stiff-legged, Archibald backed off to sit on his bed. "Name's Smifft, not Smithers. Can't stop you coming in if you want to."

Striding into the den, the chaplain planted himself firmly on the bedside chair. "Ah, that's more the ticket!"

Archibald glared murderously at the big, portly man. "No, it's not, you've just sat on Jasper and squashed him."

Rev. Miller rose in alarm. "Jasper, who's Jasper?"

Archibald craned his head to view the seat of the chaplain's trousers. "Jasper was my best lizard, I've had him all term. Now you've killed him with your big, fat bottom."

Taking his handkerchief and a nearby English textbook, Rev. Miller brushed the flattened remains of Jasper onto the floor. "My dear boy, forgive me. I'm most dreadfully sorry. Poor Jasper, I'll put him in the wastepaper basket."

Jumping from the bed, Archibald gathered up the dead lizard. He shot the chaplain a glare that would have wilted a nettle. "I'll keep him for my spells. Tongue, skin or tail of lizard always comes in useful. Not many lizards about lately."

The chaplain looked on as the boy deposited Jasper's carcass in a jar, and wrote on the label. "Spells, eh? Jolly old magic ones, I'll bet, eh?"

Archibald stowed the jar beneath his bed. "Mind your own business, my spells are private."

Chuckling, the Rev bent his head, trying to peer under the bed. "What are you keeping under here, m'lad? Lots of icky schoolboy stuff probably. Boiled tadpoles, fried worms and whatnot. Hohoho, you young rip!"

His jollity was cut short by a grubby, black-nailed finger waving threateningly under his nose. "Listen, fattie, make yourself scarce before I get mad!"

Rev. Miller had dealt with toughened soldiers in the past. He was not about to be intimidated by a snotty-nosed boy. "Now see here, Smithers, don't you dare take that tone with me. Show a bit of respect for your school chaplain, m'boy!"

Archibald's lip curled scornfully. "Respect? Get out of my dormitory, you old windbag. Go on, beat it, or I'll make you sorry you ever came in here!"

Rev. Miller stood up, then he stooped until their eyes met. "Will you indeed? I suppose you'll surround my head with flies, or slip a few cockroaches into my pocket, eh? Oh, don't worry, m'lad, I've heard all about what you did to the matron and the headmaster. That nonsense won't work with me!"

Archibald Smifft went pale with rage. "Yes, it will! I can make a big wasp sting you right on the end of your stupid nose. I can, you know!"

The chaplain's roar made the boy start with fright. "You spotty little cur, go on then, do your worst. But let me warn you, Smithers. If you do, I'll seize you and chuck you into the school lily pond, and all that gobbledygook from under your bed, too. Understood?"

Archibald sneered. "You wouldn't dare!"

Grabbing the boy by his collars, the big man lifted

him bodily and gave him a firm shaking. "You snotty little upstart, one more word out of you and I won't be responsible for my actions!"

It was the first time anyone had ever laid hands on Archibald. He squealed like a rat. Suddenly, he was afraid of the big old man. He began to whimper pathetically. "You're hurting me, put me down, please, sir!"

Rev. Miller dropped him onto the bed, nodding affably. "That's more like it, old chap. Now listen carefully. I'll return here after supper tomorrow evening. I want to see all that rubbish gone from under your bed. Also, I'd like to see a complete change in your attitude, Smithers. If not, you'll be taking a rather uncomfortable bath in the lily pond. Now, do I make myself clear?"

Avoiding the chaplain's eyes, Archibald stared at the bedspread, sniffing meekly. "Yes, sir."

Rev. Miller smiled. He patted the boy's head gently. "Good man. Now, let's have our little talk, shall we."

For the next half hour, Archibald was forced to sit and listen to the chaplain. He lectured on and on about playing the game, being a decent chap and making Crostacious's school proud of him. Archibald took it all in a subdued manner, nodding agreement with all the Rev's advice as he droned on about the dangers of evil intent, warning about casting spells and meddling in the darker side of nature.

Rev. Miller ended his discourse by saying, "There

are powers beyond your knowledge, m'boy. If you were to continue as you're going, it would all backfire on you someday. Where'd you be then, eh? Cheer up, Smithers, old lad. See you at seven tomorrow. Good-bye!"

Archibald sat listening until the chaplain's heavy, plodding footsteps receded below stairs. A slow smile stole across his spotty face, growing into a maniacal grin. Leaping up, he went into a frenzied dance around the room, his eyes glittering with villainous delight. He had just found a victim for the Ribbajack he was intent on conjuring. Old Reverend Dusty Miller, the Sky Pilot! Revengeful spite and pent-up malice poured from him like sewage squirting from a cracked cess tank. When he first heard of the Ribbajack, all he desired was to see what it looked like. Now he had a definite aim for the horror he was about to create. The removal of his newfound enemy! The moment that dog-collared old buffoon had mispronounced his name, Archibald Smifft knew the chaplain was going to be the first victim of the monster. Putting pen to paper, he began composing a verse as an aid to materialising his own personal Ribbajack.

> *O nightmare beyond all dreaming,*
> *Dark Lord of the single eye,*
> *before tomorrow's light of dawn,*
> *make the chaplain bid life good-bye.*
> *Come serve me to conquer all enemies,*

I command that you grant me this gift,
let the world fear the wrath of my Ribbajack,
and his master, Archibald Smifft!

Golden noontide sunlight flooded through the dormitory windows, the silence broken only by Archibald repeating his lines in a singsong monotone. He lay rigid on the bed, both fists pressed against his tightly closed eyes, striving to visualise his horrific creature. If there was such a thing as the Ribbajack, he would be the one to endow it with life. He was no Burmese cattle herder. No, he was Archibald Smifft. He would master the monster and bend it to his will. Rev. Miller would be only the first victim—others would follow. He would gain the power to make his Ribbajack serve him forever!

From far away, a voice entered his consciousness, distant at first, but growing to a bloodcurdling rumble.

"Master?"

Cold sweat beaded his pimpled brow; his hair stood up on end. There it was again, louder this time, clearer.

"Master! Maaaassssteeeerrr?"

From some primeval mental swamp he envisioned two gargantuan, clawlike hands materialising. They scrambled on the edge of dream-shrouded mist, then took hold and heaved. Huge serpentine arms swathed in hair and octopoid suckers emerged. A single bloodshot eye appeared, questing about frenziedly. Echoing like an organ in some satanic temple, the voice called again. "Maaaaasssssssteeeeerrrrr!"

Archibald Smifft's entire body shook until the bed rattled. He had done it, his Ribbajack was alive!

Rev. Miller slurped the last of his Brown Windsor soup. Dabbing his lips with a napkin, he announced confidently to the headmaster and matron, "I gave that young curmudgeon a piece of my mind, indeed I did! That'll teach Smithers not to dally lightly with the old Sky Pilot, eh? Magic and spells? Poppycock and humbug, if you ask me!"

Mr. Plother had already heard the chaplain's account three times. He splodged mayonnaise onto his veal and ham pie salad with renewed appetite. "I'm sure you dealt succinctly with the matter, Padre."

Mrs. Twogg buttered a slice of whole-meal bread. "Indeed, let's hope you've put an end to the whole unsavoury episode, Reverend. Would you pass the claret, please."

Rev. Miller topped up his own glass before relinquishing the wine. He began reminiscing about a similar affair involving a young subaltern in Jodhpur when the phone broke in on his narrative. The headmaster arose from his chair. "Excuse me for a moment, please."

He conversed for several moments with the caller,

then replaced the receiver with an irritable sigh. "Would you believe it? Two of our boys have recently boarded a train to Yorkshire—Harrogate in fact!"

The matron looked up from her salad. "Oh, dear, which two?"

Aubrey Plother tapped his chin thoughtfully. "All the pupils were gone by four this afternoon—there's only three remaining, Smifft, Soames and Wilton. Did you happen to see them around the dormitory, Padre?"

Rev. Miller blinked vaguely. "Afraid not, really. Ah, wait, though, I did spot two young coves before I went up there. Carrying suitcases they were, furtive, pale-faced boys."

Mrs. Twogg nodded knowingly. "That'll be Wilton and Soames."

Mr. Plother looked bewildered. "But they never applied to go home, both their parents are overseas. Where do you suppose they've gone?"

The matron stood up decisively. "We shall have to bring them back before any harm befalls them. Next train to Harrogate for us, Headmaster!"

The headmaster picked up the phone. "I'd best telephone the Harrogate Police and instruct them to hold the boys at the station until we arrive. Most inconsiderate and thoughtless of Soames and Wilton. Goodness knows what time we'll get back here with them."

Rev. Miller retrieved the claret and poured himself more. "Next train to Harrogate's at nine-fifteen, you won't get back tonight. Book rooms for yourselves and the boys at the Station Hotel. You can catch the early-morning milk train tomorrow, that'll get you back here for breakfast. Don't worry about me, I'll hold the fort here. Trains, eh, I remember back in 'twenty-eight, or was it 'twenty-seven? Old Biffo Boulton and I had to catch a train from Poonah junction. Confounded unreliable, the trains out there. Anyhow, Biffo and I had been out on a tiger hunt that same day, so we still had our guns with us, good job, really—"

The matron cut in on his story abruptly. "You'll have to excuse us, Reverend, we have a train to catch!"

The chaplain raised his glass, announcing to the empty room as the door slammed behind the pair, "What, er, by all means, you two toddle off now. By Jove, old Biffo was a card, y'know, did I tell you he had a wooden leg?"

Rev. Miller continued, unperturbed, recounting tales of himself and old Biffo in India.

Out in the quadrangle, the clock chimed 11:45 P.M. Pale shafts of moonlight replaced the day's sunrays in the dormitory windows. Archibald had not moved from his bed. He lay there, filled with an awful rapture, seeing the thing that his mind had given birth to. The Ribbajack surpassed anything that a sane, normal person could devise. Archibald Smifft had long passed the states of sanity, or normality.

The monster had curving horns sprouting from its massive blue-feathered head. A single saucer-sized eye dripped noxious fluid, glaring from above a great hooked beak. The loathsome torso, merging from its feathered neck, was coated in dirty yellow crocodile scales, right down to a pair of three-taloned feet. At either end of two long, hairy, suckered arms, the thing's lethal hands clenched and writhed, searching for something to latch on to. Its beak clashed like a steel trap as it shambled about. Archibald Smifft shuddered in villainous ecstasy as he mouthed in his sleep, "My Ribbajack! Come to your master, Ribbajack!"

As the quadrangle clock struck midnight, a bulky object hitting the floor woke Archibald. Wiping freezing sweat from his eyes, he sat upright, peering at the monstrous beast. It crouched in a patch of moonlight beside his bed, revealed in all its hideous reality.

When he could find his voice, Archibald addressed the thing. "Ribbajack, are you really here?"

Fixing him with its ghastly eye, the monster rumbled:

> *"From the pits of darkness in your mind,*
> *I am Ribbajack, born out of human spite.*
> *Say the name of the one I am brought to find,*
> *command me forever to take him from sight!"*

It stood waiting on Archibald's word, swaying from side to side, clacking its beak and clenching its talons. The dreadful eye never strayed from him. Archibald stared back at the Ribbajack, his confidence returning. After all, the thing was his creation, and here it was, standing, awaiting his command like a giant dog. What did he have to fear? Sliding from the bed, he confronted it boldly, speaking aloud:

> *"O nightmare beyond all dreaming,*
> *Dark Lord of the single eye,*
> *before tomorrow's light of dawn,*
> *make the chaplain bid life good-bye.*
> *Come serve me to conquer all enemies,*
> *I command that you grant me this gift,*
> *let the world fear the wrath of my Ribbajack,*
> *and his master, Archibald Smifft!"*

Without further exchange of words, the Ribbajack bounded swiftly from the dormitory, leaving Archibald alone in his den. Climbing back into bed, he smiled blissfully (a very rare thing for the terror of Duke Crostacious's school). Exhausted by his strenuous mental efforts, Archibald fell into a deep sleep.

At nine-fifteen on the following morn, the train from Harrogate puffed into the station. Mr. Plother and Mrs. Twogg emerged onto the platform, minus the two boys they had gone to fetch back. Tipping his cap to them, the stationmaster enquired, "What happened, sir, did the two lads give the police the slip at Harrogate?"

The headmaster replied wearily, "Not really. It appears they went off to visit Soames's aunt, quite unofficially, of course. There wasn't a great deal we could do about it. I gave them a stern piece of my mind about giving prior notice of absence. But boys will be boys, I suppose. Apart from a wasted journey, there's no great harm done. Young Soames's aunt was very hospitable. She put the matron and myself up for the night, gave us a first-class breakfast, too. Her man drove us back to the station this morning, in time for the early train."

It was not a long walk back to school. The matron strode out energetically, stretching her legs after the train ride. Mr. Plother gave a halfhearted hop-skip, trying to keep up with her. Mrs. Twogg breathed deeply.

"Ah! What a glorious day, Headmaster, not a cloud in the sky and dew still on the hedgerows. Hark, is that a lark ascending over the meadows?"

Mr. Plother's ingrown toenail was bothering him, but he tried to get into the spirit of things. "I believe it is, Matron, *Alauda arvensis*, the common skylark. Well, marm, our troubles are over. Perhaps that lark is the herald of a long, peaceful summer. The old school lies empty, boys all away until autumn term, and the Padre has solved our Smifft problem. What more could we ask for?"

The matron answered promptly. "A nice cup of tea,

Headmaster. I do hope the Reverend has the kettle boiling when we get back to your study."

On entering the school, the matron waved cheerily to the cleaning lady, who was busy mopping the entrance hall. "Good morning, Mrs. McDonald, do I smell the aroma of our chaplain brewing tea in the headmaster's study?"

The cleaner paused, leaning on her mop. "Rev. Miller ain't up out o' bed yet, Matron. I took a cuppa me own tea up t'the poor man earlier. I s'pect it's a touch of the malaria from 'is service out in India. All manner of h'ailments a body could catch out there, they say. You wouldn't catch me goin' to foreign parts. Margate'll do nicely for me, thank you."

Mr. Plother stayed the matron's progress for the stairs. "I'll pop up and take a look at the Padre. You know how he hates ladies fussing about after him. Stay down here and have a cup of tea with Mrs. McDonald."

Mr. Plother's hesitant tap on the chaplain's door was answered by a booming voice. "Enter!" Rev. Miller was sitting up in bed, looking rather flushed. The top of his nightshirt was torn, with three buttons missing. The headmaster smiled encouragingly.

"Just back from Harrogate. The two boys are staying with an aunt, no cause for alarm. Mrs. McDonald said you weren't feeling quite up to the mark, old chap. How d'you feel now, better?"

Rev. Miller snorted. "Confounded busybody, that lady. There's not a thing wrong with me. Bit of a bad dream last night, nothing more. Huh, veal'n'ham pie, and two large glasses of claret before bedtime—self-inflicted injury, as they say in the army. Feeling right as rain now, though, eh!"

Mr. Plother made the error of pursuing the subject. "Bad dream . . . perhaps you had a nightmare, Padre?"

One person was all the chaplain required as an audience. "Nightmare? Well, judge for y'self, sir. Let me tell you about it. I went to bed about eleven, never had any trouble sleeping, went off like a top. Don't know what woke me, in fact I don't know whether I was really awake—jolly strange things, dreams. Anyhow, I felt a definite presence in the room. One doesn't spend all those years in the military and not know about these things, y'know. I almost sat up straight, don't know what possessed me, but I couldn't cry out at the creature."

The headmaster shifted his gaze from a pair of Ghurka Kukri knives crossed over the mantelpiece. "You saw a creature, here, in your room?"

Knowing he had intrigued his listener, the Rev dropped his voice to a dramatic whisper. "Oh, yes, indeed I did, sir. Great hulking shuffling thing, standing there in the moonlight. The blighter looked like a crocodile standing upright. Had long arms, like a gorilla, with suckers growing on them. It was glaring right at me from one big eye, had a head of feathers and a big, ugly parrot's beak. What d'you think of that?"

A smile formed on the headmaster's lips. "Really, Padre, and how many glasses of claret did you have before retiring last night?"

The Rev's wattled neck quivered indignantly. "I resent that implication, sir. Two glasses is my limit, always is, and always has been, since I resigned my commission. How dare you insinuate that I was under the influence!"

Aubrey Plother, I.O.U.E., held up an apologetic hand. "Forgive me, Padre, it was a thoughtless remark. But what was this monstrous thing you saw?"

The chaplain nodded knowingly. "A Jibberack, or a Jabberwok. I don't recall the exact name they had for it out in Burma, but I recognised the beastie right away. I'll have to go back a few decades to explain myself, so I hope you'll bear with me, Headmaster."

Good manners dictated that Mr. Plother could not refuse. That, and the fact that he was becoming interested in the tale. "By all means, Padre, carry on, please do."

Rev. Miller continued his narrative. "Many years ago I was Padre to a garrison in Burma, stationed in the Paktai Hills. One day I had occasion to save a chap's life, Burmese fellow. It was in the floods of 'twenty-three, as I recall. I was younger and fitter then, y'know. Heard villagers wailing and shouting down by the river, so I went to investigate. Saw this poor blighter being swept away, half drowned by the floodwaters. Of course, chap like me, never stopped t'think. Dived right in, swam out, grabbed the man and dragged him bank to the bank. His name was Arif—splendid old boy, as it turned out. Anyhow, after that Arif became my man, wasn't nothing he wouldn't do for me, looked after me like a mogul emperor. We became the closest of chums, he was like a brother to me. When my term was served and I was due to return to England, poor Arif, he looked like a lost dog. I was pretty sad, too. We both knew it was the last we would see of each other.

"So there I was, waiting at the station for the coastal troop train back to Blighty. We exchanged gifts to remember one another by. I gave Arif my own personal morocco-bound Bible—wrote in the flyleaf for him, too. Arif had a medal which he always wore about his neck. He took it off and hung it around my neck. It was solid silver with a star and some ancient script engraved upon it. I was deeply touched, and asked him what it was. 'Tuan Dusty,' he said—that's what Arif always called me. 'Tuan Dusty, this is a most powerful and ancient charm. It was given to me by a very holy man. The medal will ward off the evil of a Ribbajack, and protect you from it.' "

Mr. Plother repeated the curious-sounding word. "Ribbajack?"

Rev. Miller's bushy eyebrows rose. "By Jove, I remembered it. Ribbajack, that's what they called it out there. Actually, it was a trifle embarrassing, a Church of England minister wearing some Burmese religious talisman around his neck. But be that as it may, I wore it to mark my friendship with Arif, I was proud to. I'm not ashamed to say that I still wear it to this day, see?"

Fishing inside the collar of his nightgown, the Rev drew forth Arif's medal. It was hung on braided elephant hair and looked exactly as he had described it. Rev. Miller stared out the window at the soft English summer morning, so far from Burma all those years ago. "I'll never forget old Arif, never!"

Mr. Plother inspected the medallion closely. "Tell me, Padre, what exactly is a Ribbajack?"

The chaplain looked surprised. "You've never heard of a Ribbajack? Dearie me, I'll have to complete your education, sir. Out in the Paktai Hill country, the Ribbajack was a terrifying legend. It's a monster, an ogre, a thing of immense evil, created in a person's mind. If you hate an enemy enough, they say that you can give birth to the Ribbajack from your own imagination. Once it is clear enough inside your head, one midnight hour, your Ribbajack will come alive and destroy the person you name."

Mr. Plother was aghast at the idea. "Good grief, Padre! Do you mean that a monster could be devised by the human brain which could actually take shape and commit murder?"

The medallion gleamed in the sunlight as Rev. Miller fingered it. "I do, Headmaster, and the more evil the mind of its creator, the more loathsome and fearful the Ribbajack will appear. Once its maker names the victim, the Ribbajack goes off and does his bidding. They say that when the deed is done, neither the creature nor its prey is ever seen again."

The headmaster's eyes were riveted on the speaker. "And you say you saw a Ribbajack here in this room last night. Were you its intended victim, Padre?"

Rev. Miller nodded slowly. "I must have been, because the thing went for me. It lurched forward, beak clacking, huge arms waving, staring right at me with that terrible eye. I was so helpless, the beast actually ripped my nightshirt open with its talons. Then it screeched and leaped back. I could see my medal had burned its arm. I don't mind telling you, I was in an absolute blue funk, gibbering prayers, pleas, anything that came to my lips. I was thrown back onto the pillows by some unknown force, the smell of burning flesh in my nostrils. Must have blacked out completely then. When I woke, the Ribbajack was gone. I was alone again, thank the Lord."

Mr. Plother added, "And thank that medal your Burmese friend gave you, eh? But who would want to send a Ribbajack to you?"

Both men stared at one another, the truth dawning simultaneously. "Archibald Smifft!"

Hastily donning his clothes over his nightshirt, Rev. Miller warned the headmaster, "Let's go and confront the little brute. Not a word to the matron, or the cleaning ladies. Don't want them getting upset, do we. Mum's the word, old chap!"

Luckily, the matron was sitting in the kitchen with Mrs. McDonald and her two helpers. The two men had no difficulty in slipping upstairs to the dormitory. There was neither sight nor sound of human or non-human presence. Archibald Smifft's bedsheets lay on the floor in a crumpled heap, but other than that, there was no sign of disturbance. Mr. Plother sat down on the bed.

"Well, Padre, what's our next move?"

Rev. Miller shrugged, and sat down beside him. "Not a great deal we can do, really. There's no known parents we can contact. Maybe Smithers went off like the other two boys. He might've had a relative that we didn't know about. I suppose we could contact the authorities, eh?"

Mr. Plother shook his head decisively. "We'd have the school besieged by police, press and radio reporters. That wouldn't do the good name of this place any favours. Parents would start withdrawing their boys. It might even end with us having to close Duke Crostacious's."

The Rev pondered his friend's statement. "Hmm, see what you mean. I say, d'you really want to see that young blight Smithers back here, Headmaster?"

Mr. Plother answered without hesitation. "I'd sooner have the bubonic plague, actually. A day without Archibald Smifft is a day of sheer bliss!"

"I second that, Headmaster!" They looked up to see the matron framed in the doorway. She strode in briskly. "I can keep quiet if you two can. We'll maintain the status quo, as if Smifft had never been here. Dreadful boy, I could never sleep easy at night knowing he was within a mile. Now gentlemen, to business. Headmaster, you and I will demolish this den of iniquity and dispose of it. Reverend, would you be so kind as to remove those foul decoctions from beneath the bed and empty them down the toilet. Let's get back to being an English boarding school for young gentlemen!"

Rev. Miller chuckled. "Bravo, Mrs. Twogg!"

The headmaster polished his glasses carefully, pausing before he spoke. "Er, well said, Matron. Yes, jolly well said!"

A month into the autumn term, all three were ensconced in the headmaster's study. Mrs. Twogg was pouring the Darjeeling tea. Rev. Miller passed the buttered crumpets and Chorley cakes around.

Mr. Plother gazed out the window at the trees shedding leaves of brown and gold. He sighed contentedly. "Autumn, my friends. Season of mists and mellow fruitfulness."

Mrs. Twogg dropped four lumps of sugar into her teacup. "Nothing like elevenses on a calm October day, don't you agree, Reverend?"

Rev. Miller slathered extra butter onto his crumpet. "A serenely Smitherless season, marm!"

The matron shot him a warning glance. "Don't even mispronounce that name. Remember our agreement?"

A hearty knock sounded on the study door. Rev's bushy eyebrows rose. "Hello, who's that?"

Mr. Plother called out, "Enter!"

Soames and Wilton marched in. There was a marked change in both boys. They looked healthier and happier. Young Wilton had actually put on a bit of weight. Soames had a confident, carefree air about him. He held up the jar of newts he was carrying. "Look, sir, we've been out on a nature ramble. Wilton and I caught these between us, aren't they beauties?"

The headmaster inspected the small amphibians. "Excellent work, you two. Perhaps you'd like to get some pondweed and ferns, a few nice stones, too. They'll look rather handsome in the tank on our nature table. Here, take a Chorley cake each, you chaps!"

The boys helped themselves gratefully. Wilton placed two parcels and an envelope on the table. "We met the postman in the lane, sir. He asked us to bring you the mail. Sir, could we ask you something?"

Mr. Plother sorted out the mail. Both he and the matron had a parcel, the letter was for Rev. Miller. "By all means, Wilton, how can I help?"

The boy looked rather apprehensive. "Sir, is Archibald Smifft coming back?"

Mr. Plother looked over his spectacles. "Highly un-
likely I'd say, young man. Madagascar is quite a long
way off. I don't imagine Smifft could take a bus from
there. You run along now, and don't bother your head
about him."

Soames pursued the question. "Who did he get to
take him, sir? Smifft always told us that he had no
family. Did someone claim him?"

Rev. Miller stifled a smile. "Oh, someone claimed
him, sure enough, m'boy. Actually it was an uncle,
twice removed on his mother's side. He's a mission-
ary in Madagascar. I wouldn't doubt he's training the
lad up to be a curate or something."

Peterkin Soames snorted. "Steady on, sir, that evil
bullying toad, a curate? Fat chance, I'd say!"

The matron eyed him disapprovingly. "It does not
behove us to speak ill of others. Be a little more char-
itable to your fellow creatures, Peterkin. Go on now,
off with you both!"

Looking suitably chastened, both boys left the
study. Rev. Miller heard them giggling as they ran
downstairs. "Young scamps. Boys will be boys, eh?
What's in your parcel, Matron, anything good to eat?"

Mrs. Twogg tore the parcel open. "You wouldn't
like the taste of this. It's a powder spray, repels all
sorts of insects, especially cockroaches. Did you receive anything interesting, Headmaster?"

Mr. Plother opened the cardboard box, drawing
forth a chamois drawstring bag, which he weighed in

one hand. "Silence is golden, Matron. This is another bag of rubies. I suspect our joint security lockers in the Swiss Bank must be looking quite healthy by now. As you said, Padre, mum's the word. Is that a letter from your Old Comrades Association?"

Rev. Miller was scanning the missive with great interest. "Listen to this. I took a rubbing of the medallion Arif gave me. Sent it for translation to a bod I know in the Victoria and Albert Museum. Here's what was written on my medal.

> *"Touch not the wearer of this charm,*
> *or thou wilt court disaster.*
> *O Ribbajack, return forthwith,*
> *seek out thy evil master.*
> *He whose mind first gave thee birth,*
> *this night must vanish from the earth!"*

Rev. Miller put down the letter. He went to gaze out of the window. "Thank you, Arif, my old friend."

A Smile and a Wave

Smiles and waves are given free.
They take but a moment or so,
from me to you, from you to me,
either good-bye or hello.
So bear with me, my little friend,
this story you may know,
but if perchance you've guessed the end,
just smile, and wave, and go. . . .

It was not as if Maggie liked the coat. One or two of her friends had remarked, when she first wore it to school, "Nice." This was even worse than saying it was awful. *Nice?* Nobody had said it was cool, or awesome. What can you do about a coat that your dad paid for and your mother chose? Maggie resolved to lose the offending garment, the sooner the better! So she did. Well, she hadn't actually lost the coat, just conveniently forgotten it. Now she was hoping against hope that her mother would forget it, too.

There was not much to do on a dull November Saturday afternoon. Maggie slumped on her bed, doing furious battle with her PlayStation to reach level three. Covering both ears with headphones, she caught up with the current chart vibes.

The first realisation she had of her mother's presence in the bedroom was the headphones being snatched from her ears. Mrs. Carroll stood with hands on hips. Maggie looked up at her. She knew from the body language that her mother was in her "I want a

word with you, young lady" mood. Maggie's mother
was not one to mince words.

"I want a word with you, young lady. Didn't you
hear me calling from downstairs? Have you gone
deaf?"

Maggie stared at her wall posters, explaining pa-
tiently, "I was wearing headphones. You're always
going on at me to turn the music down or put the
headphones on. I put them on so the noise wouldn't
disturb you."

Mrs. Carroll continued as if her daughter had not
spoken. "Noise, that's all it is, you couldn't call that
music! But that's not what I'm here for. Where's your
new coat? It's not on the hall rack."

Maggie made a vague gesture. "Prob'ly in the
wardrobe, how should I know?"

Closing her eyes, she listened to the wardrobe doors
sliding open. There was an irate clatter of hangers, followed by her mother's next demand.

"When did you last hang anything up properly in
here? I'm left to do all the running and tidying around
after you. Well, the coat's not in here, so where is it?
I want the truth!"

Opening her eyes, Maggie sat up slowly, turning
the music and the PlayStation off as she played for
time. But the issue was not about to be delayed. Her
mother met her eye to eye.

"None of your stories now, where is that coat?"

Maggie knew exactly where the coat was. Avoiding her mother's stare, she gnawed at the skin alongside her fingernail and tried muttering casually, "Must be somewhere, I suppose."

That did it. Mrs. Carroll took off shrilly.

"Somewhere, you suppose! What, may I ask, is that supposed to mean, eh? I paid good money for that coat. Money your father had to work hard to earn. I'd have given anything for a coat like that when I was your age. It's a lovely winter coat, and you'll be needing it when the weather gets colder. Right, you're grounded until I see that coat again, d'you understand, Margaret?"

Whenever Maggie got her full title, she knew it was pointless trying to argue with her mother. Still, she gave it a try. "But what about the ice rink? Everyone'll be there tonight."

Mrs. Carroll strode from her daughter's bedroom. "Hah! I don't care who'll be at the ice rink, because you won't if that coat doesn't turn up, so make your mind up to that, Margaret Carroll!"

The final word had been spoken, so Maggie was forced to surrender or face imprisonment. Pursuing her mother downstairs, she acted for effect, slapping a hand to her forehead as if just recalling where the coat was. "Oh, that's it! I left it in school yesterday. I remember now, I hung it over the back of my chair in the library at last period. Julie's dad was picking us both up, and he was in a hurry. So I must've dashed out to the car without the coat. Sorry, I'll get it first thing on Monday morning, honest I will."

She recoiled from her mother's prodding finger. "Sorry doesn't get it done, miss, you'll go right back to school now and get the coat, d'you hear me?"

Maggie could not credit the stupidity of her mother. "But it's Saturday afternoon, the school will be locked up tight. There won't be a soul anywhere about!"

The condescending tone in her daughter's voice made Mrs. Carroll even more determined. "I said right now, Margaret, no arguments. There's always somebody there, caretakers, workmen, cleaners, or whatever. And don't you dare take that tone with me. Now go!"

Maggie stuck out her bottom lip and pouted. Picking up her old denim jacket, she tried one last attempt against her mother's stubborn insistence. "I've been there before on a Saturday afternoon—the school's locked up tight, it always is!"

Turning her back dismissively, Mrs. Carroll left the room, calling back to her daughter, "That's your problem, miss. No coat, no ice rink tonight!"

It was less than fifteen minutes' brisk walk to L.E.T. (Leah Edwina Tranter) School. Maggie hunched her shoulders as she slouched along. Feeling very badly done to, she ruminated on life's injustices.

Only an idiot didn't know school was closed on weekends, and she had an idiot for a mother! Late afternoon was starting to fade into November twilight. Maggie began imagining fictitious scenes. A young girl (herself) run down by a car whilst crossing the road. She pictured her grieving mother.

"I should've listened to dear Maggie and left it 'til Monday. But no, I made her go. Now I've lost my only daughter, and all because of a coat she didn't even like. Oh, I'll never forgive myself!"

Hah, that'd teach her a lesson. Maggie was not too keen on being killed by the car. Maybe it would just be an injury. She pictured both distraught parents waiting in a hospital corridor. Her father, grim and tight-lipped.

"Will she be alright, Doctor, will Maggie live?"

The doctor, shaking his head. "We'll just have to pray, and wait for the results of the scan. There's a fifty-fifty chance Maggie may recover. Mrs. Carroll, I hope you'll think twice in the future before treating your daughter so harshly."

Maggie crossed the road moodily. There was not a car in sight.

L.E.T. loomed large in the dwindling daylight. It was an old greystone school, built in the 1820s. She noticed for the first time how gloomy and hostile it appeared. Still, no need to worry—it was probably shut.

Maggie's fertile imagination was working on another scheme. What if she caught a cold or a severe chill through being sent on a fool's errand? She would willingly give up a visit to the ice rink just to get even with her mother. A week off school, wrapped snugly in bed, looking pale and interesting. Toying listlessly with her PlayStation and listening to a CD whilst picking at her food.

Mentally she could hear her dad speaking downstairs. "Good grief, Annie, what were you thinking of, sending the girl out with only an old denim jacket on?"

Maggie pushed the front gates of the school driveway. To her surprise, the heavy iron-barred structure creaked open. She paused. Maybe the caretaker had forgotten to lock them. There was no sign of activity from the building, and nobody in sight. Even before she reached the entrance door, Maggie could see it was ajar. She stopped on the steps, looking hopefully about. Behind her, the gravel path with its border of withered brown bushes stood silent and forlorn. Ahead of her she glimpsed the gloomy corridor through the partially open door. Maggie was left with a choice. Either she could return home and lie that the school was closed, or she could go inside and retrieve the coat, then go to the ice rink that evening. She blew a long sigh and shrugged. Might as well go and get the coat, now she had come this far.

How different the old school looked inside! Maggie had only ever been there when it was packed with students and staff. But here it was, dead as a mausoleum,

with no heating or light switched on, devoid of everybody. Except herself. The only sound in the entire
building was the thud of her own footsteps, echoing
away down the passage. That and the beating of her
heart, which had suddenly become abnormally loud in
her ears. An uneasy feeling took hold of Maggie. She
pulled to one side of the corridor. Walking close to the
wall, she felt less exposed than if she were occupying
the centre of the floor. Crossing a side passage, which
led off to the lecture hall, something caught Maggie's
eye. A movement. She froze, keeping her face straight
ahead, but straining her eyes sideways. Down the passage, in the last weak rays of daylight, something, or
someone, was definitely moving. Also, there was a
faint rattling sound.

Moving swiftly on, she collided with the corner of
the wall. Maggie was not really hurt, but the impact
caused her to turn slightly. She was forced to face the
unknown terror. There it was, a high window with a
pale shaft of light reflecting on the opposite wall. From
outside, the overhanging branch of a tree was rattling
its leafless twigs in the wind, causing them to tap
against the glass, casting a moving shadow pattern on
the far wall. She stifled a sob of relief, glad that nobody
was there to witness her senseless panic. Taking a firm
grip of herself, Maggie moved on fast.

It was a mistake. From the end of the corridor a figure was visible, standing by the end wall, right next to
the library door. Maggie retreated immediately, duck-

ing into the side passage. This was no shadow she had
seen, it was a real person who had been coming toward
her. Wide-eyed, and with the hair prickling on the
nape of her neck, she heard her own voice calling out
squeakily, "Who's there?"

Whoever it was must be almost close to reaching
the passage where she stood. Telling herself that she
could run down to the lecture hall and lock herself in,
Maggie summoned up all her courage and peeped
around the corner. There was nobody in sight—the
corridor was empty. Peering down into the gloom, she
could make out a small movement. Then something
occurred to her. Shoving out her arm, she waved, and
dimly made out the other arm waving back at her.

It was the big mirror on the end wall by the library.

Maggie stepped out into the corridor and laughed.
Fancy almost frightening yourself to death in an
empty building because of a shadow of some twigs
and a wall mirror. It was ridiculous. Boldly she strode
down to the library, even taking time to stop in front
of the mirror and make faces at herself. Opening the
library door, she walked in, the door swishing close behind her. Maggie shrugged. All the doors in the school
did that, due to some type of hydraulic device built
over them.

At least there was some daylight in here; one wall
had large windows facing out onto the lawn and the
road beyond. Between that there was a big old
sycamore tree with a bench built around its base,

where the students sat in the warm weather to read their books. The windows had only single glazing. Maggie rubbed her hands together. It was quite chilly in the room.

Even in the twilight she could see her coat, draped carelessly over the arm of a chair in the far corner. Stupid coat, she hated the thing more than ever. Sensible, warm and totally out of fashion. She should have put her foot down flatly in the shop and refused to wear it. But as usual, her mother had won the argument. Maggie sniffed the still air. What was that smell?

Flowers, maybe, it smelt like flowers. Roses, but not freshly picked. It was not a pleasant odour—musty, cloyingly sweet. A picture of a cemetery vase filled with long-dead roses came to mind.

Trying to ignore the noxious smell, Maggie made her way across to the coat, avoiding a stepladder with a pile of old books resting on its top step. The smell increased until it filled the air with its thick repugnance. She grabbed the coat and muffled her mouth and nostrils with it. Maggie stood facing the corner, feeling rather light-headed. It was like being trapped in a dream, wanting to run from the room but unable to arouse her torpid limbs into movement.

The knowledge that she was not alone in the library stole gradually over her senses. Someone was standing in the darkening room, close behind her. Panicked thoughts jumbled about in Maggie's mind.

Whether she liked it or not, she could not stand end-
lessly there, staring at the wall and the bookshelves.
To get out of the library, she would have to turn and
confront the nameless person who was standing
within touching distance of her back. She bit hard on
her lower lip, forcing her feet, legs, her body and head
to turn in small, jerky movements. Terror rose in her
throat like bile, causing her to taste the dreadful smell
which permeated the entire room.

Maggie was not sure at first whether the girl she
was staring at was a living being or an apparition. She
was about Maggie's age, clad from neck to ankle in a
long embroidered dress of fawn muslin. Her hair was
a cloud of wispy blonde ringlets reaching almost to her
waist. The strange girl wore gloves of white silk,
elbow length. She held a single-stemmed rose, the
colour of dark blood, in her left hand. Maggie took in
all of this in one fascinated glance. But it was the girl's
face which frightened her. The skin shone like a porce-
lain doll in a museum, ivory hued and alabaster
smooth. Her eyes, intensely blue, stared unblinkingly
at Maggie, who was riveted to the spot, like a bird
mesmerised by a snake. An awful realisation numbed
Maggie's brain. The girl was blocking her way to the
door—she had her cornered.

The girl seemed to read her thoughts. She smiled
at Maggie. Her thin lips opened, revealing decayed, ir-
regular teeth. Then her mouth creased in a wide grin
as the bright blue eyes glittered insanely. It was a

smile of pure evil. Her right hand rose in a gesture beckoning Maggie toward her. The girl's chilling smile, and the overpowering scent exuding from her mouth, enveloped Maggie. She felt herself going faint, the blood in her veins turning to ice water, which broke out in a cold sweat through her skin. Fear gripped Maggie's heart in its horrific claws, then, like a dam bursting, a wild, terrified scream issued from her.

"Eeeeeyaaaargh!"

Triggered by the sound of her own fear, Maggie bolted and ran. Avoiding the girl, she fled, knocking aside the stepladder in her path, sending books spilling across the floor. For an awful second, which seemed to last an eternity, Maggie fumbled with the door handle. Then she was out of the library and tearing headlong down the corridor. The building boomed to the sound of her feet pounding the floor. Maggie's legs went like pistons as she hit the main door, sending it slamming back on its hinges as she shot out onto the gravelled path. Unreasoning horror lent wings to her feet, while her breath rasped out in sobbing gasps. Out onto the sidewalk she sped, as if the hounds of hell were on her heels. A truck rumbled by on the road, its engine noise bringing her back to the world of normality.

Maggie stumbled to a halt, teeth chattering, legs wobbling, her whole body shaking uncontrollably. But somehow or other, she was still holding tight to the coat. Maggie grasped the bars of the school railings,

staring back at the building, scarcely able to believe
what she saw.

Across the lawn, beyond the big leafless sycamore,
behind the library windows, the ghastly girl was staring back at her. Bathed in a pool of pale spectral light,
still holding the rose, still waving with that beckoning gesture . . . and still smiling that smile which en-
compassed deep, limitless evil.

Maggie turned and hurried swiftly away, her face
buried in the coat. The beautiful coat her mother had
bought for her—it smelled like home, comfort and all
the everyday things of life. No scent was ever sweeter.

It was late Saturday evening when the security patrol
informed the caretaker that his school was left un-
locked. He came out to secure it. However, he did a
quick check of all the rooms to make sure nothing
was amiss.

It was not the first time the old building had man-
aged to unlock itself, though the caretaker blamed
shrinking woodwork and the wind. He made a note to
inform the school governors.

Only the library looked as if anybody had been
there. Mr. Ryan, the caretaker, noticed the open door.
Switching the lighting on, he went to investigate.
Fallen stepladder, some old books scattered about, no
harm done really, probably a strong gust of wind from
down the corridor. The books were big, ancient, dusty

volumes from the top shelf, where reference archives were kept. He gathered them up and stacked them on a table. The last book lay open, the way it had fallen. Mr. Ryan picked it up, sat down at the table and began reading from the open pages:

The present school is built on the site of Frederick Edward Tranter's family mansion. His magnificent library was preserved and forms part of the Leah Edwina Tranter School. Leah, the Tranters' only child, died in mysterious circumstances when she was only fourteen. Many of the locals were convinced that she poisoned herself. Not much is known of Leah, save that she was a solitary girl. She was never popular with the local children, many said that she frightened them.

Leah had a private governess who was responsible for her education. She left within six months of taking up the post; no other ladies ever came to replace her. Leah spent a short but lonely life, as her parents, Frederick and Marguerite, were prominent socialites and travellers.

On returning from a tour of Europe one November, Frederick Tranter discovered his daughter's body in the library. She had been dead several days, and lay concealed behind a bookcase, holding a red rose in one hand. The servants, cook, gardener, butler and footmaid swore they had not seen her for some time. They assumed she had gone off to stay with relatives. Frederick Tranter was so affected by the death of his only child that he became a recluse.

His wife left him and went to live in Georgia, the state of her birth. None of the servants would stay in the big house with Frederick, who took to drinking heavily and staying alone in the library for days upon end. After his death it was found that he had left a will and the remainder of his money. His wish was that a school would be built on the site of his home. It would provide educational facilities for the local children. He stipulated that the building be named the Leah Edwina Tranter School, as a memoriam to his daughter.

The All Ireland Champion Versus the Nye Add

I was told this tale by my father's son,
so I'll tell it as he told it to me.
I can recite the thing word perfect,
'cos I'm an only child, you see?

The stream starts up in the mountains, and like all sensible water, it runs downhill. It's there that it joins the river and flows into the great, wide ocean. Which is how nature ordained it should. A little village stands near the riverbank with a grand view of the ocean, no more than two miles away. Now, if you sit still and listen, I'll tell you a tale which comes from that very village itself. Are you listening?

Well, if you travel anywhere in the beautiful country of Ireland, wherever people live, be it town, city or village, there's always an All Ireland Champion. Oh, it's a fact, sure enough. Each one of these distinguished folk holds the All Ireland Medal for a variety of marvellous things. Dancing, singing, leaping, jumping, eating, drinking, playing hurley, chasing pigs or destroying foxes, playing the fiddle or reciting poetry, to name but a few categories. But the fellow I'm about to tell you of is Roddy Mooney, the All Ireland Champion Fisherman. Roddy lived in a neat ould cottage near the river with his dear mother, the Widow Mooney, because he was scarce nineteen summers and not ould

67

enough to start a family of his own. Did I hear you say
that eighteen is a bit green for an All Ireland Champion? Well, I'm not given to lying, and by the beard of
the holy Saint Patrick, you'd better believe me!

Roddy Mooney had caught more fish than Biddy
Culhane had eaten hot dinners (and that's a grand ould
number if you've seen Biddy at the dinner table). Ah,
yes, to be sure, Roddy had caught trout, perch, pike,
grayling, chubb, dace, eels, lobster, crabs, garfish and
all manner of watery beasts. He'd snared them with
rod, line, net, gaff, spear and bare hands. Nothing ever
escaped Roddy Mooney. There was not a whit of space
on the walls of his ma's cottage that was not festooned
with frames, mounts and glass cases full of great
stuffed fishes. Widow Mooney, good woman that she
was, was forever dusting and polishing the trophies,
which were the proof of her darling son's skills as an
All Ireland Champion Fisherman.

But things are never as they seem, and in actual
fact, poor ould Widow Mooney was hard put to keep
body and soul of them both together. She grew cabbage
and spuds in season, and kept a few pigs and chickens
on the plot behind her neat cottage. They never had
fish, because Roddy hated the taste of scaled things.
There were times when his dear ould mother would
have eaten the leg off a tinker's donkey for a nice bit
of fish. But Roddy wouldn't dream of bringing home
fish to cook. He kept the finest specimens for his dis-

play, but all the rest he threw back or chopped up for bait. So, despite the fact that he was a champion angler, Roddy Mooney was a great lazy lump of a lad who would not lift a finger to help his mother, and her a widow, too. But aren't I the one for rattlin' on. Let's get down to the story, and a queer ould tale it is, I promise you!

So then, there's little Mickey Hennessy, one fine golden summer noon. Ten years old, and a slip of a boy, with no more meat on him than a butcher's pencil. Fishing by the river, armed with no more than a crooked stick, a yard of string and a bent pin from his ma's apron with a worm dangling from it (the bent pin, I mean, not his ma's apron). Mickey fancied himself as a Junior All Ireland Champion. When along comes Roddy Mooney himself.

"So then, me little man, what are you doin', tryin' to drown that worm?" says Roddy.

Says Mickey, looking serious, "I am not. Sure, I'm after tryin' to catch meself a Nye Add!"

Roddy looks at little Mickey as if he was christened with a vinegar bottle and had his brains completely destroyed. "A Nye Add, is it? An' what in the name of all that's good an' holy is a Nye Add?"

So Mickey, being the grand lad that he is, explains all about Nye Adds (though I'm not sure if that's the plural). "Barney Gilhooly told me that a Nye Add is a fine pretty lady who lives under the water. Barney used to be a sailor, y'see, an' he's the man who'd know. He said he saw many a one of them when he was off the coast of Calatrumpia years ago."

Roddy sits himself down on the bank, next to Mickey. "Barney Gilhooly, that terrible ould fibber? All he ever sailed on was the village pond, and all he ever saw was through the bottom of a whisky bottle. So, what did Barney say a Nye Add looks like?"

Little Mickey pulls in his line. The worm is drooping, so he casts it back again for a further bath. "He said that a Nye Add is half a woman and half a fish, but a rare beauty. He said sometimes they used to come out onto the rocks, combin' their hair an' singin'. Sure, Barney said that the sound could drive a man mad completely!"

Roddy laughs. "Then Barney must've heard the Nye Add singin', 'cos he's as mad as Rafferty's pig with a bee in its bonnet. Now let me get this straight, Mickey. A creature that's half fish an' half a woman, but not altogether either. Livin' under the water, an' comin' out now and again to comb her hair an' sing, just to drive fellers daft. Sounds like an underwater banshee to me."

"Aye, she may be just that," says Mickey. "Sure, I'll let you know when I catch one an' get a good look at her."

Roddy does no more than glance at Mickey's fishing gear, then he laughs. "Mickey, me little tater, you've got more chance of of seein' O'Hara's goat singin' in the church choir than ye have of catchin' the creature. What makes you think there'd be such a thing in this ould river?"

"Because I saw one here not an hour since," says Mickey.

"I think you've been sittin' out too long in the sun. So where did ye see it, pray tell?" says Roddy.

So little Mickey explains. "Me ma sent me for a duck egg, for me da's tea. I was walkin' along the footpath by here when I sees Mulligan's dog. Sure, he was creatin' an awful racket, barkin' an' howlin' at somethin' in the water. So I goes to see what all fuss was in aid of. That's when I saw the Nye Add swimmin' around under those bushes by the far bank. Well, she saw me, an' dived straight down an' hid, so she did!"

Roddy looks over to the spot Mickey had indicated. Something occurrs to him which gives him pause to chuckle. "Are ye sure it never had a fish's head an' a lady's bottom?"

Little Mickey does not like being made fun of. "Arr, away, ye great eejit, I saw it with me own two eyes. The top was woman, an' the bottom was fish. 'Twas a Nye Add, she looked just like Barney Gilhooly said she should!"

The lad seems serious, and Roddy is getting curious. "Just over there, ye say?"

As Mickey nods, Roddy picks up a stone about the

size of his fist. He heaves it out into the river and hits
the very spot where Mickey had seen the creature.

The stone had scarce struck water, when a great
fluke-shaped tail rises and slaps down hard on the surface of the river, drenching them both with spray.

Little Mickey Hennessy wipes the water from his
eyes. "That was her tail. Now will you believe me,
Roddy Mooney?"

The All Ireland Champion Fisherman grabs little
Mickey's shirtfront, causing half the buttons to pop
off. "That's no Nye Add nor water banshee! All I could
see was its tail, but that's a fish, the biggest ever seen
in Irish freshwater, I'll bet. A shark, or a dolphin, or
some kind of deep-sea big-game fish found its way upriver from the ocean. Mickey, ye darlin' little man,
will ye do somethin' for me?"

"I will if ye stop tearin' the shirt from off me young
body," says Mickey. So Roddy tells him the plan.

"Stand guard here an' watch in case the fish moves.
I'm goin' home for my anglin' tackle. I'll be back before ye know it, so I will!"

The good Widow Mooney is chucking turf bricks onto
the fire when in dashes her son like a nun with a bee
in her bonnet.

"Sit ye down, me luvly son. I've mashed some grand
taters an' buttermilk up for your tea," says his ma.

But the All Ireland Champion is already packing all his tackle in a wicker creel. Maggots, hooks, lines, ledgers and floats. "Sure I haven't the time t'be sittin' round feedin' me gob, Ma. There's a fine big ould fish needs catchin'!"

He seizes a selection of rods and sundry other poles, then grabs his lucky hat, the one with all the bright-coloured flies stuck in it. Jamming it on, Roddy knots the hat strings under his chin and goes tearing out of the door, with his ma shouting after him, "I'll put it in the oven to keep warm for ye, son!"

So then, there's Little Mickey marching up and down the bank with his twig over his shoulder, keeping guard over the spot, as Roddy arrives in a cloud of dust. Mickey salutes like an Enniskillen Dragoon. "Sure I've not seen it move, so it must still be there!"

Roddy Mooney starts unpacking tackle, talking to himself the way that All Ireland Champion Fishermen do. "Now, will the beast be takin' a woolly nymph, or a red hackle weaver? I'd best use me good split-cane rod, an' a heavy line. Where's those musket ball ledgers, an' a decent float? Mickey, will ye stop pacin' up'n'down like a half-paid officer? Get that maggot tin an' sling some ground bait out."

Like most small boys, Mickey loves to play with

maggots. Shoving his hand into the battered tin, he rummages about happily among the squirming mass of maggots. "Ah, sure, I don't know whether or not Nye Adds eat these."

Roddy squints as he knots the red hackle tight onto his line. "Will ye give over, there's no such thing as a Nye Add. That's a monster fish in there, big enough to take the gold cup at the Bantry Bay All Ireland Reel Off. Aye, an' I'm the very man who's goin' to catch it. Now will ye give up messin' with those maggots an' throw them in the water!"

Mickey slings out two handfuls, shouting, "Lord ha' mercy on your little maggity souls!"

Roddy whips his rod back and forth several times, then casts out expertly. The hunt for the creature is on.

But fishing, as you all well know, is a lengthy business. Three hours later the pair is still sitting on the bank edge, with no luck thus far, not even for an All Ireland Champion. Of course, not knowing the grand, exalted title held by Roddy Mooney, the honour of the occasion is probably lost on any fish swimming in the river.

Four, five, six hours go by. Apart from a small eel and a half-dead roach, nothing decent comes near Roddy's hook. Little Mickey has lost interest in the proceedings. He's trying to catch a dragonfly with Roddy's keep net, but most dragonflies are craftier than most little boys. So Mickey gives up the chase and sits back down with Roddy.

"Do ye not think 'twould be better goin' home for

somethin' to eat? It's gettin' dark now, we could come
back tomorrow, eh?"

Roddy Mooney concentrates on his unmoving float.
"Sure, ye stand a better chance at the night fishin'.
That's when the big fishes come up to feed."

Little Mickey's stomach rumbles like a cart going
over cobblestones. "Have ye not got any ould sam-
midges under that hat, Roddy? I'm fair famished for a
bite!"

"All Ireland Champion Fishermen don't need food
when they're fishin'," says Roddy.

Suddenly, out of the dark waddles Bridgie Hennessy, Mickey's fine big mammy. She fetches him a
clout that knocks him sideways, and roars at him,
"Where's the duck egg for your da's tea, ye Hessian de-
serter? Where've ye been all day an' half the blessed
night?"

Regaining half the sense he had before the clout,
Mickey explains, "I been fishin' for a Nye Add with
your man Roddy Mooney."

His distracted mammy lifts Mickey off the ground
by the seat of the trousers. "Fishin', is it? I'll fish ye!
Your da an' your twelve brothers'n'sisters have been
out scourin' the country for ye!"

Mickey is hauled off home, keeping up a midair
conversation with his mammy. "What's for supper? I
could eat an ould horse!"

They vanish into the darkness, with Bridgie Hennessy bawling like a Mullengar heifer.

"There'll be no ould horses for you, ye hardfaced melt! A taste of your da's belt an' straight up to bed, that's all you'll be gettin' for your crimes!"

Sitting alone in the dark night, Roddy feels happy as a donkey in a strawberry patch as he waits to catch the fish of his life. He wonders if anyone has ever gained the title of Double, Supreme or Majestic All Ireland Champion Fisherman. The summer night is quiet and warm, with not a breeze to stir the calm air. From behind the cloudbanks, a dusty gold moon emerges to dapple the river with pale shadows. Roddy's eyelids droop. He stifles a yawn and settles his back against the cane hamper. Even All Ireland Champions have to sleep, ye know.

A plip and a small splash close to the bank where he is sitting causes Roddy to wake immediately. He never moves, but directs his gaze to the water, beneath which his feet are hanging over the river edge. He sees the huge flukes of the tail waving enticingly, a mere inch from the surface. Beyond the tail he glimpses a fraction of the thick scaled body underwater, but it is impossible to see more. By the sword of Finn McCool, this is one big fish!

But the dilemma is, how to catch it? The fish is sure to swim off if he makes a sudden move. Roddy Mooney is a grand man for making up his mind quickly in angling situations. He decides the prize can only be taken with a gaff. Now if you're ignorant as to what a gaff is, I'll further your education. A gaff is a

huge, sharp steel hook, bigger than those you see at
the butcher's with meat hanging from them. The gaff
is lashed tight, with stout cord, to a pole. Gaffing is a
most unsporting and, in some regions, illegal way of
catching fish in freshwater. Gaffs are generally used by
poachers to hook fish, mainly salmon, as they leap up
to climb waterfalls and weirs. It is a cruel thing, because the gaff usually strikes the fish right through its
body. The fish wriggles in agony until the angler dis-
patches it by striking its head with a heavy object.
You have to be skilful and swift with a gaff or you lose
the catch.

But Roddy Mooney has to have the big fish. So,
keeping still as possible, he reaches behind with one
hand, inch by inch. Locating the gaff where it has been
lying on the grass behind him (Little Mickey had been
using it to dig for worms), Roddy finds the leather strip
he has knotted through a hole in the handle. Sliding
the strip about his wrist, he takes a good grip of the
pole. The fishtail is still waving invitingly, almost
touching his boot soles. The All Ireland Champion begins raising the gaff with painstaking care. One strike,
that is all Roddy knows he would get the chance of.
Slowly, slowly, like a snail climbing a wall, he raises
the gaff, until his arm is fully stretched. The wicked
steel point of the hook is perfectly balanced, ready to
strike.

Roddy Mooney strikes like lightning. However,
whatever is under the water strikes back like greased

lightning, which is much faster, probably because of
the grease. The gaff is seized hard by its curved hook,
and Roddy gets hauled, hat over hobnails, into the
river. You understand, he has no option but to go, as
the gaff is looped around his wrist. Now, you can believe this or believe it not, but it is no big fish which
yanks the All Ireland Champion into the drink.

Beneath the water, everything looks like an enchanted world. Moonlight shining through the river
gives the entire scene an unearthly glow. In the soft,
pearly green radiance, waterweeds and fronds sway
gently seaward with the current. But Roddy ignores
the charming vista completely. His attention is captured by the girl who is holding his gaff hook, and a
fine big specimen of fishy maidenhood she is, to be
sure. From tail to navel, her lower half is covered in
silver scales, which I suppose most underwater folk
take for granted. She has thick greenblack hair, which
covers her upper half modestly down to the fishy bits.
From top to waist, she resembles a human being, except for her hands, which have webbed fingers and
long curving nails. The smile she gives Roddy near
frightens the life out of him. I say that because she has
no lips to speak of, merely a wide gash of a mouth,
which curves downwards. Her teeth are gleaming
white and sharply pointed—there are lots of them, far
more than you or I have. Now isn't that odd, but even
stranger are the two gills on the sides of her jawline
that keep opening and closing like they have a life of

their own. Her eyes are solid jade green marbles with just a black slit at the centre of each one, showing no white whatsoever.

Roddy feels an urgent desire to be back home in the neat little cottage with his ma. He tries pushing himself upward to the surface, but the fishgirl tugs on the gaff, pulling him back down. She reaches for Roddy's hat, which is covered with colourful flies and strapped beneath his chin. He puts out a hand to stop her. She knocks the hand away and lets out an almighty shriek of protest.

"Yeeeeeeeeeeeeekkkeeeeeekkkk!"

Like a red-hot darning needle, the sound goes through Roddy's eardrums. He opens his mouth in shock, letting the water rush in. Poor ould Roddy, I hear you say, but that is only the start of his troubles. The fishgirl shoves him flat on the riverbed and sits on him!

She pulls the hat from his head and begins unhooking the flies from its brim. Pinned beneath her, Roddy shuts his mouth tight, and bubbles stream from his nostrils. Evidently, this causes the fishmaid some grand amusement. Switching her attention from the hat, she jiggles up and down on Roddy's stomach, shrieking with laughter at the bubbles that are streaming from her captive's nose.

After a while, Roddy's mouth pops open, his last remaining gasp of air bursting forth. *Burrloop!*

The fishgirl loses interest in him and starts looping

the coloured flies into her long tresses. They look rather weird, but pretty nevertheless.

Just then another fishy female comes on the scene. She is much bigger and older than the girl—in fact, it is her mammy. She deals the daughter a whopping blow with her powerful tail, sending her flying, or should I say floating. Grabbing Roddy in her strong webbed hands, she whooshes him straight to the surface. With a single mighty heave, she flings him high up onto the bank, as though he is no more than a wet dishcloth. The unconscious All Ireland Champion lands with a grand swishing flop, facedown, with his head hanging over the bank.

Streaking back down to the bottom, the big fishwife begins giving her daughter a good ould scolding. The young one bares her teeth, hissing and shrieking as she argues back with her mammy, the way that some fishmaids do. Now, to the layman, the entire argument might sound like a load of submarine caterwauling. But to a student of underwater jargon, the gist of the noises goes roughly like this:

"Arrah, ye daft little shrimp. What've I told ye about fishin' for leggy ones? They're nought but trouble!" says the mammy.

Then her daughter replies, "Sure, 'twas him that was tryin' to catch me. Did ye not see all those funny little bubbles comin' from the leggy one?"

The mother gives her another tailwhack.

"Ye destructive little sardine, have ye not got the

sense of a barnacle? You'd probably like to have destroyed that leggy one. Aye, he'll not be the same again, if he lives. Ah, well, I suppose we'll have to be goin' back to the ocean now. Selfish little haddock, ye've ruined our river holiday completely. An' ye can get those things out of your hair, faith, 'tis tatty enough without all that nonsense!"

At this, the fishmaid gives an impertinent pout, just like one or two young madams we might know.

"It's not fair, Mammy, sure I was havin' a grand ould time up here in the river. I'm not wantin' to go back to the ocean."

The mammy isn't about to be putting up with teenage tantrums, though, wise fishwife that she is. "If ye had the brains of an oyster, you'd know we won't get a moment's peace here when they find the leggy one. There'll be leggies here in their droves by tomorrow, splashin' about, hurlin' rocks and probin' 'round with great poles. They'll muddy the water up until our gills are filthy. 'Tis always the same, so come now, move your tail, we've got to go."

Well, away they go downstream, with the young fishgirl still complaining. "But Mammy, that big fat dolphin will be after me again. I can't stand the great gobeen, forever squeakin' and smilin' that big stupid grin of his."

Like all good mothers, the mammy gets the last word in. "Listen, Miss Picky-fins, ye could do a lot worse than that nice dolphin. He comes from a respectable family, an' he's very intelligent, too. So get along with ye before I skelp the scales from your tail!"

So, it is the Sunday morning of the following week that I must move on to, are ye listening? Father Carney has finished the mass, and like the saintly man he is, he goes off to visit his sick parishioners. His first call is at the neat little cottage of the Widow Mooney. The reverent man accepts a cup of tea and visits the poor woman and her son, the former All Ireland Fishing Champion. With a rug about his legs, Roddy sits in an armchair, staring out into space, his face all pinched and thin, the skin white as a corpse. He has heard and seen nothing since that fateful night, living in a sort of permanent coma.

Well, there is not much the father can do. He says a few prayers for Roddy, then blesses him before enquiring of Mrs. Mooney, "Has he not moved at all, spoken or anything?"

The widow serves the priest with a slice of soda bread spread with her very own fresh churned butter. She wipes both eyes on her apron and sniffs aloud. "Ah, sure, I'm completely distracted, Father, me son's like the livin' dead. Night an' day he's as y'see him now, alive only by the mercy of the Lord. 'Tis a sad burden for a mother to see her darlin' son in such a miserable state."

She straightens a lock of Roddy's hair and wipes his nose on her apron corner. Father Carney looks away, saddened by Widow Mooney's grief. It is then he sees the crowd of village onlookers jamming the doorway and windows to see what was going on inside. Shoving on his battered hat, he reaches for his knobbly blackthorn stick. "We must trust to the power of prayer, Mrs. Mooney. I'll drop by again this evening, after benediction."

Striding out, the priest confronts the crowd of gawping faces angrily. "Have ye no homes to go to? Be off with ye, now. 'Tis not a penny peepshow, there's a grieviously sick person in there! Give the lad's poor mother some peace, for pity's sake!"

Mary Creeley, the village gossip, purses her lips shrewdly. "Father, is it true that Roddy Mooney's had a spell cast on him by a water banshee?"

The good man shoots her a glare of disgust, then moves off, surrounded by curious villagers all wanting to hear what he has to say concerning the All Ireland Fishing Champion. "Wash your mouth out, woman, that's a sinful thing to say. Who's been filling your head with such nonsense?"

Barney Gilhooly winks at the priest and smiles slyly. "Ah, well, Father, there's some knows what they knows, an' there's things not better mentioned. That's what I always say."

The priest halts and shakes his stick at the man. "Hold your foolish tongue, Gilhooly! Who knows what, eh? An' who listens to the tales of snot-nosed urchins or tattlin' ould gossips that should know better!"

The crowd stands cowed by the reverent man's wrath. But Mary Creeley, who would have the last word with a hangman, calls out in a whining voice, "Ah, sure, nobody tells us anythin', Father. We're left entirely in the dark, with only the words of one witness, the child who was the last to see Roddy Mooney on that day."

Father Carney's stern eye seeks out little Mickey Hennessy. "Witness, indeed! Ah, ye make me sick, all of ye. Believing the ramblings of a child who'd say anything for a sweet! Listen to me now, I'll tell you the truth as only a priest can."

Little Mickey Hennessy ducks behind his mammy's shawl as the good father thunders out at his errant flock. "Holy Mother Church forbids belief in all pagan superstitions! If you attended your services more often, you'd all know that. Hah, standin' outside of Gilligan's pub, tellin' fairy stories, ye should be ashamed of yourselves as grown men an' women! Water banshees, is it? Leprechauns, boggarts, sprites, willow the wisps, phantom coaches an' pots of gold at the rainbow's end. Do ye not know that folk with a bit of sense an' education laugh at such things?"

Father Carney strides off in disgust, leaving the chastened villagers gazing at the ground in silence.

But that ould Mary Creeley, she is like a dog with

a bone, she will not leave it alone. She wails out piteously at the saintly man, " 'Tis yourself that's right, Father, sure, we're knowin' nothin'. Simple ignorant folk is what we are. I'd say it's your duty as our holy priest to tell us, what really happened to poor Roddy Mooney?"

Holding back his irritation with remarkable fortitude, Father Carney gives his explanation of the affair. "Have ye not got the sense the good Lord gave ye? Your man was out fishin', an' he fell into the river. Somehow or other, he was trapped underwater, by the weeds, or mud, or even some waterlogged branches. Poor Roddy was so long tryin' to free himself that his brain was affected by the loss of breath an' all that water he swallowed. But by the mercy of Heaven he lived through it all. Though his brain was addled, an' he's not the grand feller we once knew, an' that's why Roddy Mooney's the way you see him now. Let that be the last word on it. An All Ireland Champion Fisherman he might've been, but an All Ireland Champion Underwater Escape Artist he was not!"

So there you have it, the terrible tale of poor ould Roddy Mooney. It happened almost sixty-five years ago. Now, whose explanation are you to believe, that of a priest or a ten-year-old boy, little Mickey Hennessy? As for meself, I believe the lad, and I'll tell you why.

Every midsummer since, at the night of the full moon, the boy has gone down to the very spot on the riverbank where Roddy was taken. Aye, all those years, an' he still goes there. Listen, I'll not be telling anyone but yourself this, for fear of being laughed at. Mickey still sees the Nye Add lady return, to look for Roddy Mooney. Of course, being the wise man he is, Mickey keeps well away from the river's edge. But over all that time he has learned to understand the creature's language, though he cannot speak it, because Mickey's no great shrieker. The fishwoman told him that she's neither water banshee nor Nye Add, she's called a Kelpie. I think that she fell in love with Roddy, because she returns there every midsummer, hoping some moonlit night to see him. Ah, she's a sad ould thing now.

Well, I've told you the tale now, so I'll go on me way an' bid ye good day. But it's a true story, an' if I've told you a lie, then I'm not seventy-five years old next birthday, and my name's not little Mickey Hennessy.

The Mystery of Hunia D'Este

THEY SAY THAT BEAUTY IS ONLY SKIN DEEP,
it's a fact that's very well known.
So, answer me this question—
how deep is the beauty in stone?
And whilst we're at this little game,
pray tell me please, what's in a name?

Girls admired Jason Hunter, boys envied him, and not unusually, Jason loved himself. He was a tall, handsome boy with thick blond hair, golden tanned skin, teeth like pearls and heavy-lidded hazel eyes.

Jason was not overly intelligent at school subjects. However, he was adept at most sports, and excellent at running. He was the best sprinter in the school for many terms. As every student knows, this excused him a multitude of faults.

Jason possessed a languid manner and a sarcastic wit. Most folk went out of their way to please him. His group of peers laughed readily at his jokes, and were unanimous in their condemnation of any thing or person that displeased him. Even teachers were wary of offending him, since it was a sure way to make themselves unpopular with the students in school.

Have you got the picture now?

Right. Jason Hunter was the perfect teenage bully!

It was the Friday morning at the start of summer term heralding the Inter Schools Running Finals on the following Saturday morning. Jason was certain to win the one-hundred-metres sprint. The place in the school trophy cabinet was already reserved for the cup he would bring back. This would be added to the three cups he had gained in previous terms, all engraved with his name. The quick glory of the one-hundred metres was more suited to Jason's temperament than the two- or four-hundred-metres. Nobody dared to mention that it was because he lacked the stamina, or determination, to try for the longer events.

Jason sat on the main school entrance steps, surrounded by his followers. He watched everybody coming to school, amusing his group by singling out certain unfortunates as the target for his caustic comments. "Hi, Tommy, who cut your hair? Tell us who did it, and we'll go along to his shop and beat him up for you."

The crimson-faced victim of Jason's acerbic wit hurried into school, followed by howls of laughter. Jason picked on a fat girl next, she made an easy mark.

"I love the colour of that skirt, Betty."

She smiled gratefully. "Thank you."

Jason remarked aloud to his cronies, "I used to have a tent that colour, wonder where it went. Don't suppose she'd lend me it to go camping, do you?"

They followed one after another, each having to run the gauntlet of Jason's remarks.

"Morning, Ella, I see you got your new braces. That's funny, has anyone noticed the old railings round the bus stop are missing? Come on, Ella, give us a smile. No, on second thought, keep your mouth shut. The cops might be looking for those railings. Don't cry, we won't tell them."

That was the day the new girl arrived. She stood out from all the rest as she approached the steps. She was very tall and had long dark hair, which hung down almost to her waist. Her face was pale, her eyes a bleak grey. She wore a simple black outfit of sweater and jeans. Moving with a catlike grace, she came closer, oblivious as to what was in store for her.

Mal Blake, one of Jason's close confidantes, rubbed his hands gleefully. "Look what's coming this way, must be a new girl!"

Running a comb through his hair, Jason rose casually. "Leave this to me, I like them new and dumb."

As she reached the bottom step, he stood blocking her way. Jason smiled lazily at the girl, who was standing on the step below him. He uttered a single greeting. "Morning."

Their eyes met. She replied dismissively, "So clever of you to have noticed."

She moved up to the next step, level with him. Jason had to raise his eyes—the girl stood a good three inches taller than him. Brushing carelessly past her would-be tormentor, the new girl went straight into school. Mal stood up, chuckling.

"Pretty smart, eh, Jason?"

Slipping a foot behind Mal, Jason gave him a shove,

which sent him back down in a sitting position. The bully snarled at him, "Who asked you, big mouth?"

Jason's angry glance roved around the others, who averted their eyes. Nobody wanted to cross Jason Hunter; besides being scathing, he could be violent. He stepped over Mal as the buzzer sounded for everybody to go indoors.

"She's too smart for her own good. You just wait and see, I'll soon cut her down to size!"

From the rear of the assembly hall, Jason could see the tall girl standing out on the front row. Mrs. Dysart, the assistant principal, addressed the students. It was all the usual stuff about hard work, good manners, friendship and a sense of purpose. Following the initial pep talk, Mrs. Dysart singled out the new arrival.

"We have with us this term a new student. I'm sure you will all try your utmost to make her feel welcome. Her name is Huma D'Este."

Jason ducked his head, gave out a loud snort of derision and shouted, "Human who?"

In the hush which followed, Jason stared accusingly at a boy standing in front of him. It was Tommy, the one whose hairstyle he had mocked earlier on. Jason spoke out in a shocked tone.

"That wasn't a very nice thing to say, Tom!"

Mrs. Dysart gave the unfortunate Tommy a piece of her mind in front of the whole assembly. However, the new girl was not looking at Tommy, she was staring directly at Jason. Something in the gaze of Huma D'Este's strange grey eyes wilted the smug smile from Jason's face. He looked down at the floor, dumbfounded and angry that he could not stare back at her. Who did she think she was, giving him that look? Still, he reckoned, it was early in the day yet. Plenty of time to reduce her to a figure of fun in front of his admirers. Everybody knew what was going on, they had all witnessed Jason destroying those he had taken a disliking to.

Recess found Jason on the steps, surrounded by his retinue. An air of expectancy hung over them as they awaited their leader's next move. One of his informants, Mal's friend Carlene, came hurrying out of the school. "Jason, the Human's coming!"

They had taken to calling Huma "the Human" since Jason had invented the name at assembly. When she emerged, the new girl did not seem in the least put out at the thought of the bully awaiting her. Jason swaggered up to her, raising his eyes in mocking awe.

"Hi, big girl, what's the weather like up there?"

Her reply hit him like a slap in the face. "Oh, it's fine. Would you like me to lift you up so you can see, little man?"

Turning on her heel, Huma wandered back into the school, stopping in the doorway and fixing him with a slow stare from her hypnotic grey eyes. Jason was tongue-tied. He stood there with the laughter of the others ringing in his ears. Why was it that he lost his famous wit whenever she spoke or turned her gaze on him with those eyes?

One or two of the faithful deserted Jason, going inside before the break ended. He heard their smothered giggles. " 'Would you like me to lift you up so you can see, little man!' Haha, she certainly shut him up with that one!"

"Yeah, and Jason just stood there and took it!"

"Huma's well able for Jason, if you ask me. Hahaha!"

The buzzer sounded. Jason turned to the remainder of his cronies, a bright tinge rising to his cheeks. "Wait'll lunch break, I'll make her sorry she ever met me!"

Standing out of range of Jason's kicks or shoves, Mal grinned. "I'd like to see that."

Jason made his way back into class alone, wondering, Was that a scornful note he had sensed in Mal's voice? A small group of girls, whispering about something, broke up as he entered the room. Jason did not pay attention to a single word of the lesson. Huma D'Este . . . his thoughts could focus on nothing else. He rehearsed the lunchtime scenario. This time things would be different, oh so different.

Jason spotted the new girl as he sidled into the school canteen. She was sitting amid a group of girls, chatting animatedly. Some girlish giggles came from the company. Were they laughing at him? He shot them a look of disgust, but Huma seemed to be ignoring him.

Jason strode swiftly and purposefully across. Placing a heavy hand on Huma's shoulder, he pressed down. Feeling he had the advantage of looking down at his victim by keeping her in the chair, he enquired loudly, "Huma—what sort of a name's that? Huh, it makes you sound almost human!"

Even though he was pressing down hard on the tall girl's shoulder, she stood up straight with no apparent effort. Again, he found himself locked within the stare of her riveting grey eyes. They were cold and bleak as rainwashed stone. Huma spoke his name as if it were two separate words.

"Jay son! What's in a name, Jay son? Is your father a bird? It certainly sounds like it. Jay son, son of a jay!"

Mr. Forshaw, who was on canteen lunchtime duty, had been watching the body language of the pair. Sensing trouble, he made straight for them. "Excuse me, could somebody tell me what's going on here?"

The moment was lost. Jason muttered something about going to the counter for food, and slouched off.

Mal and Carlene had saved a place for Jason. They moved over as he sat down, placing a slice of pie and a can of cola on the table. Mal could hardly wait. "Well, what did she say?"

Jason shrugged. "Nothing."

Carlene looked at him disbelievingly. "You must

have said something to each other, we saw you talking just before old Forshaw arrived. What was it?"

Fighting for control of himself, Jason clenched his teeth. He gripped the can of cola so forcefully that it crushed, sending liquid squirting all over his slice of pie. "Nothing! Just keep your noses out of it! We said nothing!" He stormed off from the table, knocking his chair over.

Carlene turned to the retinue, who were sitting at the opposite table. "Well, what do you make of that?"

There was a chalk cartoon sketched on the math class blackboard when Jason arrived. It showed a bird with huge muscle-bound legs and a human face, which resembled Jason pretty closely. Just so there would be no mistake as to the identity of the bird, a balloon issued from its mouth, enclosing some words:

"Duuuuh, I'm a jay's son!"

Jason could not face Huma's eyes. He turned on the rest of the class, yelling, "Come on, who drew that, eh?"

Mr. Wentworth, the math teacher, entered at that moment. He brushed the offending image from the board, calling over his shoulder, "Keep the noise down, Hunter. Right, pay attention, class, decimal conversion . . ."

His voice faded into the distance as Jason locked his eyes on the back of Huma D'Este's head, sending waves of hatred pouring at her. The plastic ballpoint he was gripping snapped in two halves; a vein in his forehead throbbed like a drum. That girl! One way or another she would have to go. There was no room in his school for Huma D'Este!

Jason wracked his brain for a solution throughout the afternoon. She was very smart, so he would have to be smarter. More careful, too. He must pretend to call a truce, make friends. Then, when she was off guard, he would destroy her. Nobody treated Jason Hunter like that and got away with it.

Fate is fickle, and the company of unwilling friends short lived. Jason Hunter had his first experience of this as he came out of school that day. His customary group of hangers-on, even Mal and Carlene, had gone over to the enemy. They were standing on the steps, gathered around Huma, chatting animatedly. Jason controlled his rage, telling himself that after he had humiliated the tall girl today, and captured the one-hundred-metres sprint cup on Saturday morning, everything would change. He would be the star once more, the sole, undisputed leader of the pack. As he approached them, he could hear the muted laughter, someone even made a birdlike squawk. But Jason shrugged it off. He had laid his plans.

He stood in front of Huma, pretending to shuffle his feet awkwardly, keeping his head down. It was a ploy

which had always worked well with parents and
teachers. Flicking his blond hair aside, Jason gave
Huma a charmingly sorrowful smile, playing the little boy just right. "Er, Huma, can I have a word with
you, please?"

She turned the remorseless grey eyes upon him.
"It's a free country, you can have as many words as
you please."

He felt his jaw tightening, and checked it. "Er, I
just wanted to say I'm sorry I joked about your name.
I hope I didn't embarrass you too much."

As her eyes bored into him, she smiled conde-
scendingly. "Think nothing of it, Jason, you didn't embarrass me, you only embarrassed yourself by your
own bad manners and lack of wit."

It was the ultimate insult to Jason, being put down
like an ill-mannered child in front of everybody.
Something inside him snapped. He swung his open
hand at Huma's face, roaring, "Shuttup, you smart-
mouthed—"

The tall girl avoided the slap by knocking Jason's
hand up. As he stumbled forward, she pushed the back
of his neck hard. Jason tumbled down the steps, falling
facedown on the ground. He scrambled to get up, but
was sent back down. Huma had the flat of her foot
firmly between his shoulder blades.

Leaning down on him, her grey eyes hard as gran-
ite, she warned him, "Stay down, Jason, you're on

your own now, so leave it alone and stay clear of me, do you hear?"

He struggled, but big and strong as he was, the tall girl's foot held him there. A man's voice called from the doorway, "Stop that this instant, stand still, you people!"

Mr. Knipe, the athletics coach, and Mr. Wentworth, the math teacher, came bounding down the steps.

Jason felt himself released from the restraining foot. He struggled up, fists clenched, trying to get at his enemy. He was hauled back by the huge, hairy hand of Mr. Knipe. Mr. Wentworth stood between Jason and Huma.

"Fighting with girls now, are we, Hunter?"

Wiping dust and tears from his face, Jason pointed at his adversary. "She started it!"

A clamour arose from the onlookers. Mr. Knipe held up his free hand. "Anyone not wanting to do twenty circuits of the school field, go straight home. Now!"

The area cleared as if by magic—the coach was a man of his word. Mr. Wentworth looked at Huma, shaking his head. "Not a very good start for your first day at school, miss."

The girl's grey eyes were soft and disarming as she smiled ruefully at the teacher. "It wasn't serious, sir, we were only messing about."

Mr. Wentworth, captivated by her, smiled back.

"Messing about, eh? Well, there's no real harm done. Go on, get along home now, and no more messing about."

Huma flashed both men an extra-warm smile. "Thank you."

When she had gone, Mr. Knipe turned to Jason. "What've you got to say for yourself, Hunter?"

The culprit avoided his eyes. "Nothing, Coach."

There was an awkward silence as Knipe looked him up and down. "Not hurt, are you? Fit for the race tomorrow?"

Jason assured him, "I'm alright, Coach, I'll win the cup."

Knipe nodded. "Make sure you do, and no more of this wrestling with young ladies. See you tomorrow."

He released Jason, watching him jog off toward the gates. "Pity we don't have martial arts for the girls. She looked as if she had the better of Hunter there."

Mr. Wentworth turned back to the school. "Hmm, we could do with a few more like Huma D'Este. That Jason Hunter's a born bully, but he got his comeuppance from her. I quite enjoyed seeing him getting a taste of his own medicine."

Friday night was humid and still. It was already one-thirty in the morning, and Jason was still unable to sleep. He lay on top of his bed, his mind a jumble of seething emotions. Thoughts of the past day's events nagged at his brain. Huma D'Este, the one fly in his ointment. A single tall girl with odd-looking eyes. She was responsible for making him look foolish, forcing him to lose face in front of the whole school. A sudden thought occurred to him. Huma D'Este was still tormenting him. Supposing he lay awake, unable to think of anything but her? He would lose sleep, and turn up at the Inter Schools Trophy tomorrow tired and listless, unable to run properly or concentrate on the race. Everybody would be there, all eyes would be on him.

Jason rose. He sat on the side of his bed, staring out the open window at the hot, still night. Something must be done if he were to regain his former glory. That was it! He would drive all thoughts of her from his mind and think only of the task ahead. Hurrying off to the bathroom, Jason set the shower until it gushed forth tepid water. A good, long shower, followed by a peaceful night's sleep. He took a long, luxurious shower, then towelled himself slowly. Wrapping the towel about his waist, he stood in front of the mirror, running his hands through his thick blond locks, admiring his physique and good looks. Telling himself he was a natural winner, Jason went back to bed. Ignoring the duvet, he lay down and composed his mind until sleep overcame him. Deep, dark, comforting sleep.

Yet the eyes of Huma D'Este came to haunt Jason's dreams. Distant at first, but advancing slowly through

misty vales of slumber. Growing larger and more lu-
minescent until his whole being was immersed in
their spell.

"Come to me, Jason, come to me."

The husky voice was insistent, a promise, a command, a plea and a challenge. "I know you, Jason, you
must come to me." It was unlike any dream he had
ever experienced.

With the towel knotted about his waist, Jason was
running barefoot across his own garden. Taking the
low hedge in an easy leap, running, running. Along
the nightdark avenues and crescents, pools of light
coming and going as he passed beneath streetlamps.
Grass verges felt soft beneath his feet, asphalt paths
smooth and still warm from the day's heat. Running,
running.

"Come to me, Jason, hurry, I am waiting, Jason,
waiting!" He increased his pace through the hushed
neighbourhood, his muscular legs performing like a
well-oiled machine. The eyes floated before him, un-
blinking, mysterious, twin beacons guiding him to his
destination.

Now he was leaping a low fence, weaving through
flower beds, skirting a miniature fountain. Jason's
dreamlike stride took him past a patch of white rho-
dodendrons, across an area of ornamental ferns, beyond a final screen of high-trimmed privets, to a large,
old-fashioned house, silent and gloomy in the moon-
less night. Without any conscious knowledge of

whither his feet were taking him, he loped up the broad stone steps.

Jason passed through a black lacquered front door, which stood ajar. Making his way across a vestibule with windowpanes of lilac and pale blue glass, he padded heedlessly along a high-ceilinged entrance hall. On the weaving patterns of its terrazo floor stood several tables of skeletal delicacy, each one graced with urns containing verbena, aspidistra and miniature parlour palms. The huge grey eyes guided him onward to a rich curtain of Tyrrhenian velvet, then into a vast circular room.

She occupied a white stone throne, which stood on a dais in the centre of the chamber. Clad from neck to ankle in a gown of carmine silk, her feet encased in dainty golden sandals, and her brow circled by a slim coronet of burnished silver. The tall girl resembled some priestess out of ancient legend. Her eyes stared down at him, framed by alabaster skin and raven hair. Not knowing why he did it, Jason knelt down on one knee and spoke her name in hushed tones. "Huma D'Este!"

The regal gaze never wavered. "That is a name I permit those who do not know me to use. I will reveal my real name to you in a while, should you wish to hear it, but beware, Jason Hunter. Look around you, is my temple not beautiful?"

The chamber was ringed with alcoves. In each was a stone plinth, like a small Grecian column. A lifesize marble statue had been mounted on every one. They were of young men wearing little save loincloths. Every figure was superbly sculptured, looking either heroic or sporting in turn. Classical Greek titles were graven on the plinth of each statue. Huma D'Este named them.

"Here is the mighty Hercules, there, Orpheus, the poet. Next to him stands Paris, son of King Priam. See, Achilles the warrior, Odysseus the wanderer, Narcissus the beautiful and Arion the musician."

She reeled off one name after another as Jason gazed, awestruck, at the beautiful lifelike details of the works. "Theseus, son of the god Poseidon, Ganymede, the handsome cupbearer, Bellerophon, rider of the winged Pegasus, and Leander, who swam the Hellespont to woo the maid Hero. These are my wonderful collection, the males of legend, whose names the ages have not dimmed!"

Jason scanned the statues, eleven of them in all. The only one he had ever heard of was Hercules, and that was via movies and television. However, being no student of classical mythology was not a bar to his admiration of the amazing sculptures.

"They look great, but I counted eleven. That's an odd number . . . is there one missing?"

Huma closed her eyes, the ghost of a smile creasing her lips. "Ah, you've noticed. The empty plinth is right behind you. One of the curtain folds is obscuring it. Go and see."

Jason turned to the curtain, then folded it aside, revealing the empty plinth. Peering at it, he tried to decipher the name carved there in Greek characters. "I can't make out this funny writing . . . suppose you can, though."

Huma sat back and sighed blissfully. "Ah, yes, I know who will stand there for eternity. He will be the son of Aeson, rightful king of Iolcus, the one who was reared by the centaur Chiron. Do you know of him?"

Jason shrugged. "I don't know any of those foreign names."

Huma spoke teasingly. "No, I didn't suppose you would. Some of the most beautiful bodies are seldom endowed with the keenest of minds. Let me give you a clue. This young man was captain of a ship named the *Argo*, he stole the fabulous Golden Fleece of Colchis. Now do you know him?"

Jason was awake now, the dreamlike trance seeming to have left him. He felt silly, standing here in the dead of night, clad only in a towel and his briefs. And there was the girl whom he had known for only a day, sitting on a throne, all dressed up and surrounded by statues. Now she was starting to mock him again. The fact that her eyes were closed made him bold. He spoke insolently. "No, I don't know him, and I couldn't care less. I'm getting out of this stupid old place!"

He was about to run off when the eyes of Huma D'Este sprang open, riveting him with their piercing stare. Her voice was harsh and commanding. "Fool, you should know the one I speak of. His name is the same as yours. Jason! When I saw you yesterday, I knew that you were the final piece of my collection!"

The towel was wet and clammy about his waist. Jason felt frightened and helpless in her presence. He could not tear his gaze from the girl's eyes. They were growing larger, more overpowering, ugly red veins threading out from their corners.

He could hear his own voice, a fearful whisper. "How would you know what this Jason looked like? He must have died hundreds of years ago."

Huma's face was changing, the skin taking on a purplish hue. Cracks began pitting it, things were moving beneath her eyebrows, down the sides of her nostrils and along her jawline. The luxurious black hair weaved itself together into a nest of writhing snakes. Jason watched in horrified fascination, as if his eyelids had been frozen—he could not shut them. Now her mouth opened, a thin forked tongue sliding out.

"We of the Immortals have seen many things in the centuries which are dead and gone. Nothing escapes us."

Jason's limbs began trembling uncontrollably. "Wh-Who . . . are y-you?"

Two black scorpions emerged, framing her eyebrows. She leaned forward, spitting viciously, "My name is the same as that of my mother, Huma D'Este.

That is the name I use for ordinary mortals who have not the wit to unravel it. You are too stupid to realise, but if you changed the letters of Huma D'Este around, you would know that I am called The Medusa! Look upon me, my Jason. I am nightmare come to life, my gaze is sent from the dark regions of Hades to turn living men into stone. Gaze on me and attain eternity, my Jason!"

The eyes of The Medusa became twin pools of evil. Winds like the searing heat from a furnace blasted the chamber, scorching the entrance curtain to ashes, behind which the wall was sealed tight as a tomb. Screams of lost souls ripped through Jason's eardrums. With the terrifying vision of The Medusa robbing him of his sanity, he turned and ran. Round, round and round the exitless room he sped, spurred on by her brain-splitting laughter. Trapped like a moth in a cage with a hawk.

Then he froze! There was no more Jason; the hunter had been well hunted. All that remained was a cold, beautiful statue of Jason, caught in the act of running, every detail captured in lifeless white marble.

It had been many years since Carlene and Mal Blake were teenage sweethearts at school. They had remained together, happily married now for fifty years. Their three children had children of their own, who called Carlene and Mal "Nanna" and "Grandad." The family got together to present the old couple with a wonderful golden anniversary gift, the vacation of a lifetime. One month's cruise of the Greek islands. Blue sky, warm sun and an even bluer sea, with every luxury that the SS *Hellenica* could provide for American tourists.

Two weeks into the cruise, it was a glorious afternoon on one of the old Mediterranean islands. Passengers clicked cameras and zoomed in through video lenses on lined peasant faces, olive trees, whitewashed houses and a small village square with sunlight bouncing off the hosed-down cobblestones. After a fine alfresco meal, complete with glasses of the local wine and a bouzouki music serenade, they boarded a bus, which took them up into the mountains to explore an ancient villa and its grounds. It was a walled edifice comprised of timelessly beautiful gardens and an imposing house, which had once been a fortress in the fifteenth century. The guidebook reliably informed tourists that the building contained an art collection.

Age had been kind to Carlene Blake; she was still a slim and lively little lady—unlike Mal, who was grey-haired, overweight and had breathing trouble. Added to that, he also suffered from angina. Carlene helped her husband to keep up with the party as they walked around the estate, though she could see he was clearly in need of a rest when they entered the house. They found a bench in a shaded entrance porch and sat down, leaving the others to follow the guide inside.

Mal immediately went into his noontide nap. Carlene brushed his wispy grey hair back, removed his sunglasses and tipped a straw trilby over his eyes. She left him, with his big stomach gently rising and falling, and went off after the party inside the house.

She could hear them off somewhere in a side room full of Greek Orthodox artworks and religious icons. They moved on upstairs, their chatter receding in the distance. The hushed atmosphere was pleasantly serene. Carlene lingered on in the cool stone-floored main hallway. On one wall, there were glass cases with tiny bronzes of Minoan bull dancers, which did not interest her greatly. However, farther down there was a magnificent collection of twelve marble statues representing the manhood of classical Greek mythology. Mal still had the guidebook in his pocket, so she wandered along, trying to identify each one with little success. The names carved on the base of the plinths were a complete mystery to her. However, she did identify Hercules, or Heracles, as he was known in this part of the world. Hercules was easy, they had small figurines of him on sale in the ship gift shop. It was the last statue that arrested her attention—a very handsome boy in a running pose. He had a wrapping about his waist, which Carlene was thankful for. These Greeks, some of their statues did not even have a fig leaf for cover!

Against all the house rules, she ducked under the ornate tasselled rope separating the public from the exhibits. The handsome running boy interested her. Standing precariously on the base plinth, she reached up and touched the intricately wrought face. It reminded her of somebody. Glancing up at the heavy-lidded eyes, Carlene experienced a sudden flash of recall. Mal would think her foolish when she told him, but the features were a perfect likeness of the boy from their school days, Jason Hunter.

They had seldom mentioned him over the years. Jason, the good-looking one. He had vanished one summer night, all those decades ago. Nothing was ever heard of, or found again, despite the statewide coverage, the police searches, publicity posters and rewards offered by his anguished parents. Jason Hunter had just disappeared from the face of the earth, leaving no trace behind.

On tiptoe, Carlene peered closely at the statue's features, cudgelling her mind to remember how Jason had really looked. Oh, dear, it was all in another time, another place, all those years back. Sounds of the ship's party returning to the main hall caused her to skip nimbly down and under the guard rope.

Carlene waited until the group passed before tailing on at the rear. As they left the hall, she took a last look back at the running boy. No, he had a more noble and classical form than Jason. All she really recalled was his face, fixed in that lopsided sarcastic smile of his. Jason had used it on herself, and Mal, many times when they were young. Jason Hunter had not been a very nice young man anyhow. She and Mal had never really liked him.

Before she woke Mal, Carlene tipped the Greek guide with a few drachmas. He had a nice smile.

"I see you look at the statue of Jason, he is pretty, yes?"

She nodded politely. "Oh, they're all exquisite statues."

The man pointed back at Jason, confiding to Carlene, "One time an Australian lady, she bend down and look up the cloth he wears around his waist, yes. Her friends ask her what she see. Hahaha, she say, 'I see nothing, only a label that says 'Fruit of the Loom.' Haha, good, yes?"

Miggy Mags and the Malabar Sailor

TYRANTS ARE ALL SHAPES AND SIZES,
their unfortunate victims also,
though when one realises,
'tis a heartening thing to know—
gallant heroes will still appear,
to give aid in the hour of need.
This tale, from my hometown, you may like
    to hear,
of a very odd champion, indeed!

Miguela McGrail went barefoot in the summer and wore clogs in the winter. She was never sure of her age, whether it was eleventeen or twelveteen. Atty Lok, the Siamese cook, was largely responsible for this, always making jokes about figures and words. He would tell her she was born in fourteen fifty-eight instead of eighteen fifty-four. Miguela, or Miggy Mags, as she was known around the wharves and quays of Liverpool's dockland, knew that Atty was just pulling her leg. She would make a funny face at him, and the little man would grin back at her, from ear to ear.

Athanasius Tang Lok was one of the few real friends Miggy had in the world, so she was constantly harassing him with questions. "Alright then, what was the day an' month of me birth?"

Carving bacon from the half of a salted pig, the cook judged how much he required for breakfast. "You borned in fourteen fifty-eight, on umpty-ninth of Nextober, that be true!"

Miggy climbed up on the potato sacks, watching a

Norwegian whaleship sailing in through the locks. "You're a terrible fibber, Atty Lok. Last time you said it was on the sixty-seventh of Junevember. Anyhow, when's my dad's boat comin' in, eh?"

The Siamese pared off another rasher, slightly pink, but mostly fat. "Pancake Friday, on Christmas Sat'day, prob'ly."

Miggy was about to reply when a rough voice from the chandlery startled her.

"Miggy! Have you trimmed those lamps an' cleaned the winders yet, yew idle liddle mare?"

The girl grabbed a pail of water and some rags from the stone sink, shouting a reply. "In the minnit, Uncle Eric, I was just havin' me brekkist!" The sound of clumping boots approaching sent Miggy staggering outside, splashing water from the pail as she went.

Eric McGrail was a big man—big footed, big fisted and big bellied. He strode into the kitchen, wiping lamp paraffin from his hands on the greasy apron tied round his middle. Atty nodded toward the front door.

"Miggy be out there, working hard, plenty hard!"

A blue scar on Eric's forehead puckered as he glared at the cook. "Who asked yew? Get on with yer work, an' don't be cuttin' those bacon rashers so thick. Yew'll be the ruin of me!"

Outside, Miggy was perched on a rickety old lard box. One of the two big brass storm lamps, which hung from either side of the door, was receiving her earnest attention. She polished energetically at the red glass lamp panes. Each night both lamps were lit, providing illumination for all to see the sign over the front door.

MERSEY STAR.
SHIP'S CHANDLERS AND
BOARDINGHOUSE.
CLEAN BEDS. QUALITY FOOD.
REASONABLE RATES.
CASH ONLY. NO TRADE OR CREDIT.
PROP. E. MCGRAIL.

Uncle Eric scowled up at Miggy. "When yer finished there, girl, get some sandstone an' scrub the steps. Anyone asks fer me, I'll be in the Maid of Erin. I've got important business there. Make sure those lamps are prop'ly trimmed, or I'll trim you if they ain't!" He gave the lard box a small kick, causing Miggy to hang on to the lamp bracket, lest she fell.

Uncle Eric pulled off his apron, tossing it inside the door. A moment later he was off down the cobbled dock avenue, clad in a dirty blue saloon jacket two sizes too small for him, a high-waisted pair of serge trousers, shiny with wear, with a broad brass-buckled belt holding them up.

Eric swaggered along like he owned the entire Liverpool Dock Estate. Tilting his billycockbowler hat forward, Eric took a ha'penny clay pipe from its band. He lit it and puffed out a rank cloud of Burmah Thick Twist tobacco. He would not return until late. Drinking all day with his cronies in the Maid of Erin was always important business.

Later that morning, Miggy was scrubbing the white pine dining tables. She scraped away with a broken knife blade at a cigar burn. Men often rested their cheap, thin cheroots on the table edges. A seaman came in, toting a gunny bag, tossing it on the counter. He ordered a room and a meal—some bacon and eggs. Sitting at a corner table, he waited. Miggy brought him a bowl of tea, some cruets and cutlery. After Atty cut two thick slices of bread, he set a big iron frying pan on the stove, calling out cheerfully, "Bacon'n'eggs ready pretty soon, sir, not long, you bet!"

The man was a bosun. Removing his peaked cap, he placed it on an adjacent chair. Immediately Miggy recognised the cap badge. Two curved Indian swords, surmounted by a green letter *B*—the Bengal Line. She bobbed a respectful curtsy at the bosun. "Beggin' y'pardon, sir, but me dad's a sailor, aboard the *Bengal Pearl*. Would you know him, sir? His name's Patrick McGrail."

The bosun nodded. "Aye, girl, your dad's a good man, I've sailed with him. The *Bengal Pearl*, ye say? I docked last night with the *Bengal Queen*, she's my ship. I reckon you should see your dad soon, the *Bengal Pearl*'s about a week behind us."

Miggy dashed to the counter, yelling, "Did ye hear that, Atty, me dad's comin' home next week!"

The cook handed her the bosun's breakfast. "Nex'

Monday Tuesday, eleventy-second of very good Friday, eh?"

The girl's clogs clattered on the floorboards as she danced up and down with joy. "He'll be here next Wednesday, y'great daft codfish!"

Atty waved his big bacon knife at her. "Daf' codfish you'self. Give man food, don't drop plate!"

Miggy served the bosun his meal, asking him twice about when the *Bengal Pearl* would berth at Liverpool, just to make sure she had the facts right. For the remainder of that day, her heart sang and her feet skipped continuously. Her dad was coming home soon!

Atty Lok watched her fondly. He could not help mentioning to the bosun, "She be happy when father return, but cry a lot when he sail away again. Very sad for little girl, very sad."

The bosun of the *Bengal Queen* shrugged. "Sailors must follow the sea to earn their bread. Seagoin' men should stay single, no wife or kids, like me."

The Siamese cook shook his head. "Not good for young girl to have no mamma, an' father always away on ship."

Later that night, Atty lay on his mattress in the cellar. He listened to Miggy singing from behind the blanket which curtained her quarters off.

> "'Twas a cold an' frosty mornin' in November
> . . . vember,

> *an' all of me money, it was spent, spent*
> *spent!*
> *Where it went to now I can't remember . . .*
> *member,*
> *so down to the shippin' office I went, went*
> *went!*
> *Paddy lay back, Paddy lay back,*
> *take in yer slack, take in yer slack,*
> *take a turn around the capstan heave aport*
> *. . . heave aport.*
> *Oh, bow ships stations boys be handy . . . be*
> *handy,*
> *for we're off to Valparaiso round the horn!"*

The sound of heavy footsteps and the creak of the cellar door caused her to fall silent. The curtain was wrenched back suddenly. Uncle Eric stood there, swaying. He held a quart bottle of porter in one hand, a half bottle of rum protruding from his pocket. Eric, who had lost money gambling at pitch and toss, was in a sour mood.

Miggy hid herself beneath the old Royal Navy blanket which covered her mattress. She heard him stumble as he knocked out the ashes from his pipe against a raised boot heel. Her uncle regained his balance and belched loudly.

"No use hidin' under there, girl, you cut that caterwaulin' an' get t'sleep! Oh, an' a little bird told me yer father's homeward bound. I wouldn't get too joyful if'n

I was you. That footloose brother o' mine won't be back too long. Quick turnabout an' ship out agin, that's Paddy for ye. Aye, an' I'll tell ye summat else, he'd better come up with more money this time. Huh, leavin' me 'ere to watch out for his brat, after that Spanish bit he called a wife went gallyvantin' off. An' him, sailin' away to where ye please, while I've got to look after yew. Givin' you the best of everythin', an' teachin' yer a respectable trade, too. An' little enough I gets fer it!"

Eric lurched off, waving his pipe stem at the cook. "Bring me brekkist at nine sharp tomorrer, ye heathen, an' make sure the tea's well sugared, or I'll sling yer in the dock!"

After her uncle had gone upstairs, Miggy peeked out from under her blanket. Atty, rigging up her curtain again, gave her his usual cheery grin. "Not worry about him. Eric like cracked temple bell, alla time making silly noise. Sleep now, father be back soon."

The days passed slowly. Every chance she got, Miggy sat out on the quayside chains, watching for a sight of the *Bombay Pearl* coming upriver. The young girl was so taken up with her father's return that she often forgot some of her chores. Late each night, Uncle Eric would totter down to the cellar, pretty much the worse for drink. He would bellow and roar at Miggy, calling her an idle little mare who was eating him out of house and business. Miggy hid beneath her blanket, weathering the verbal storm in silence.

One night, Eric began shouting that he was going to

teach her a lesson. He started to unbuckle his belt when a sound from the cook's pallet caused him to turn. Atty Lok was standing there, sharpening his big bacon knife on an oilstone. The eyes of the little Siamese man were flat and dangerous as he gazed unblinkingly at the fat, drunken bully. Uncle Eric took the warning, muttering thickly to himself as he staggered back upstairs.

At six in the morning of the following Wednesday, the *Bombay Pearl* sailed gracefully through the lock gates on a floodtide. Miggy Mags was already dashing barefoot along the quayside as her father's ship tied up against the west wall. She met him before he was halfway down the gangplank. Paddy McGrail swung his daughter off her feet, hugging her as she planted kisses on his stubbled cheeks.

"Ahoy there, Miggy, me darlin', just look at the size of ye? What a lucky ould salt I am, to be welcomed home by such a charmin' princess!"

Carrying his seabag over one shoulder and toting a bulky-shaped burlap sack in his hand, Paddy ambled along the quay with a jaunty western ocean roll. Miggy's skinny legs skittered back and forth as she skipped circles around her dad, peppering him with questions. "How long are you home for? Oh, I hope it's ages an' ages! Will you still be on the *Bombay Pearl* an' the India run? What's in that sack, is it somethin' for me, is it, Dad?"

Paddy's eyes were twinkling, he pretended to look

dizzy. "Will ye be quiet an' still for a moment, Miggy, me girl, you've got your poor father worn-out already. Hoppin' round like a cat on hot cinders, an' chatterin' on like a cageload o' magpies. Have mercy on a simple sailorman."

She giggled at his pitiful expression. "Alright, Dad, I'll be good, honest I will!"

Clasping both hands primly, Miggy lowered her eyes and straightened her back, as she had seen well-to-do college girls doing on their way to church services.

Paddy could not help smiling, he was so fond of her. "That's better, me darlin', now listen to me. I'll be in Liverpool four days, while the ship's unloadin' some gear. Then I've got to sail with the *Pearl* up to Greenock in Scotland. We're dischargin' most of the cargo there, then comin' back here for another seven days to get laden again. So, I'll be home four days, gone another six, then home for a week. Good, eh, Miggs!"

Miggy figured out the total time she would spend with her dad, laughing. "Atty Lok will say it's eleven-teen days. But it's the longest you've been home in ages. What have you got in the bag, Dad? Please tell me."

Paddy shook his head. "Is that Siamese cook still around? He's a nice little feller, but he's teachin' you your figures all wrong. Proper schoolin', me girl, that's what ye need—it's eleven days, not eleventeen."

Miggy shrugged. "I know that, Dad, I can count right enough. But you still haven't told me—what's in the sack?"

Paddy gave her a broad wink. "I'll tell ye later, darlin'. Look, we're home. There's me brother Eric,
waitin' on the step t'greet me. He looks like a bulldog
chewin' a wasp, but don't tell him I said that."

Paddy nodded affably to his scowling elder brother.
"Eric, great t'see ye again, mate!"

Eric sucked on his clay pipe, and spat out sourly, "I
suppose ye'll be wantin' some brekkist. Come on inside.
An' you, girl, get yourself into that kitchen. There's men
need feedin', an' not a dish washed in the place. Shift!"

Paddy stroked his daughter's unruly brown curls.
"Go on, darlin', do as your uncle Eric says."

Both men watched her go indoors. Eric stowed the
pipe in his hatband. "Huh, just like her mother, hungry as a wolf an' lazy as a sow. By rights she should go
to the parish."

Paddy's eyes blazed with anger. "No daughter o'
mine is goin' to end up in the parish workhouse. I pays
you good money for Miggy's keep, ye can't deny that!"

Eric slouched inside. Indicating a vacant table to
his younger brother, they both sat down. Paddy saw
Miggy wearing an apron many sizes too large for her.
She was carrying out breakfasts to the waiting lodgers.

Eric rapped a grimy finger on the tabletop. "I been
waitin' to have words with ye about the girl. She ain't
a baby no more, Paddy, she's growin' up fast. I'll be
needin' an extra twelve bob off ye. Things bein' what
they are, I can't afford t'keep her on the money ye give
me. Have ye seen the price o' things nowadays?"

Paddy stared incredulously at his brother. "Another twelve shillings?"

Eric scratched his stomach, replying offhandedly, "It's either that, or she goes to the parish."

Paddy counted out money from a small bag strung round his neck. "There, that's what I usually pays ye, plus the extra twelve bob. Miggy goes to the parish over my dead body. Right?"

Eric watched as he slammed the money down on the table. He skimmed it quickly into his trouser pocket and stood up. "Right, I'm off to the Maid of Erin, got some business there. Stow yer gear in the cellar, I won't charge ye. 'Tis better than sleepin' aboard ship."

Without a backward glance he sauntered out the door, off to the pub and a long day's drinking.

Miggy shed her apron and ran to sit in the seat her uncle had vacated. Atty Lok appeared, carrying a trayful of food, which he brought to the table.

Miggy spread her arms grandly. "Brekkist for two, please!"

Paddy shook the Siamese cook's hand warmly. "Atty Lok, ye old grubroaster, how are ye, my friend?"

Atty continued pumping Paddy's hand up and down. "Paddy 'Grail, old cockleshell, I fine, how you? Both eat up now, plenny good special I make for you an' daughter. See, eggs, bacon, sausages, toast, molasses an' plenny tea!"

Paddy grabbed his knife and fork eagerly.

"All the way from Bombay I've been dreamin' of a good Liverpool feed. Salt horse, ship's biscuits an' weevils in the hard tack, that's what I've lived on for six months. Atty, you're as merciful an' kind as the Buddha himself!"

The cook sat and watched until they had finished. "Much good chow, eh?"

Paddy slapped his lean stomach. "Fit for a Mogul of India. Now come with me, I've got something to show ye both."

Between them they carried Paddy's gear down to the cellar. Placing the bumpy sack on Miggy's old navy blanket, Paddy undid the drawstring.

"This is a present for you, Miggy, me girl. Wait'll you see this!" Some cotton waste and ship's ration scraps tumbled out of the sack, then a small head peeped forth.

The girl stared wide-eyed at the beast emerging from the sack. It had a pointed nose, little whiskers and a pair of eyes which shone like black diamonds. Slightly smaller than a tabby cat, the creature had short legs, a long thick tail and a bristly silver-grey coat, almost blue where the lantern light caught it. Standing on its hind legs, it licked at Miggy's fingers, which had traces of molasses sticking to them. It was not afraid of the girl, nor she of it. Miggy smiled.

"Oh, isn't he lovely, Dad! What sort of animal is he?"

Paddy stroked its back with one finger. "This, me darlin', is the Malabar Egyptian. Right, Atty?"

The Siamese cook spoke in reverent tones. "That feller mongoose, bravest snake killer in alla world. You wait here, I get friend mongoose some food!"

Whilst Atty was gone, Paddy explained to his daughter about the animal. "Y'see, Migg, this feller ain't no common mongoose. He comes off a very special strain. His father an' mother were both prize serpent slayers, bred from rare stock. His bloodline is a mixture of two kinds o' mongooses. Malabar, an' Egyptian ichneumon, the bravest there is. They're also the most lovin' an' faithful of pets, ask Atty, he'll tell ye."

The cook returned with an egg, which he gave to Miggy. "Hold mongoose, blow in his face gently, soft now."

She did as he instructed. The mongoose leaned close to her mouth, its nostrils twitching. Atty nodded.

"He know you now. Crack egg a little, put it on floor for mongoose feller. He like egg pretty good."

Miggy cracked the egg slightly. Liquid leaked from it as she placed it on the floor. Putting the mongoose down next to it, she spoke quietly. "Come on, Sailor, this is for you."

The little beast leaped on the egg, holding it with its paws and attacking the shell with razor-sharp teeth. Paddy McGrail watched his daughter stroking the mongoose as it lapped up both yolk and white like a hungry kitten. "Sailor, eh? That's a good name for him."

Miggy nodded. "Well, he sailed with you, Dad, all the way from India. What do you think, Atty?"

The cook shook his head. "No, should be called Lascar, that name for Indian sailor. Lascar!" He reached forward to stroke the creature's nose with one finger. It snarled, baring its teeth warningly. Atty pulled his hand away quickly.

"He loyal to you now 'til fifty-sixth of Foreveryear. Best he be called Sailor, he British citizen now. You take care of Sailor, he take care of you, ho, yes!"

Miggy scoffed. "How could a little fellow like him take care of me?"

Atty Lok sounded deadly serious. "I tell you, missy, mongoose fear nothing, not scared of poison serpent or death. He protec' you good!"

Sailor had finished his egg. He looked up from the well-licked shell fragments at Miggy. Folding him in her arms, she stroked him lovingly. The mongoose snuggled up to his new owner, making rusty little noises of pleasure.

Paddy McGrail cautioned his daughter, "Don't be carryin' him round an' pettin' him like that. I've got a feelin' that Eric doesn't like animals of any kind, especially foreign ones. Keep Sailor out of sight when your uncle Eric's around. No sense invitin' trouble, darlin'."

Miggy heeded the warning, it made good sense. "Don't worry, Dad. I'll make him a little nest behind my bed, and I'll only bring him out when Uncle Eric isn't in." Whilst she talked, the young mongoose gazed up into her eyes, as if listening intently to every word Miggy said.

Every one of the four days her dad was home, Miggy Mags rose early. She fed Sailor on bacon rinds, crusts spread with molasses and the odd cracked egg, which Atty left out for her. She went about her tasks with a will, the object being to get them out of the way so she could spend time with her father. Everything went well until the third day. Paddy had taken Miggy for a visit aboard the *Bengal Pearl,* a delightful day out for her. Her dad's shipmates, both crew and officers, went out of their way to make her happy. Most of the men were bachelors and had no children of their own. They were enchanted with Paddy's young daughter. Miggy was given a tour of the vessel, from stem to stern, by two whiskery old salts. A wheelhouse officer even let her turn the massive brass-bound mahogany steering wheel, allowing her to wear his peaked cap. She was served afternoon tea in the crew's mess with the captain, doctor, purser and all hands attending. Miggy was treated to ham sandwiches, Madeira cake and Ceylon tea. The captain showed her how to stick out a little finger when holding the delicate Satsuma china cups, which he had provided for the occasion. The purser asked her to pour tea for them, chuckling as he referred to her as "Mother." It was early evening when they came ashore, Paddy swaggering proudly alongside his young daughter. Miggy had some coins and handcrafted trinkets donated by her dad's shipmates. It had been a day to remember.

But disaster awaited them on their return to the Mersey Star Boardinghouse.

Atty Lok came hurrying up the quayside to warn them. "Eric have much sick belly, he come home early from pub. Ho, yes, big bad mood, you stay out of Eric's way until he go up to room an' sleep!"

The cook was about to tell more when Eric Mc-Grail appeared at the door. His face was ashen. He crouched, clutching his stomach as he roared, "Where've ye both been all day, eh? Leavin' a poor sick man to fend for hisself. Fine family you two are!"

Paddy pushed Miggy behind him as he enquired about his brother. "Eric, are you alright, mate, what ails ye?"

The boardinghouse keeper allowed himself to be escorted inside by Paddy and Atty. He lowered himself, groaning, into a chair, where he sat wiping slobber from his chin. "I could've been dead an' laid out, for all youse lot care. I was took bad in the Maid of Erin, an' had t'find me own way home. It musta been somethin' that foreign heathen put in me brekkist this mornin'."

He bent forward, wincing, as he pointed at Miggy. "Either that, or I've been infected by that rat you been keepin'. Where is it now, ye filthy liddle scut?"

Paddy answered, defending his daughter. "Easy now, Eric, you're sick. Miggy wouldn't keep no rat as a pet, she's scared of rats. There might be some outside, on the wharves an' under the piers. Talk sense, mate, whoever heard of anyone havin' a dock rat indoors as a pet, eh?"

Sweat beaded on Eric's pasty brow as he heaved himself up. "Oh, ye think I'm out o' me mind, talk sense, is it? I'll talk sense right enough. I saw the thing with me own eyes, a rat, near big as a cat the damned thing was. It was skulkin' round in my cellar when I went down to look for the girl. Come an' see for yerselves!"

Lifting the trapdoor behind the kitchen counter, he beckoned the trio to go down ahead of him. "Go on down there, I'll show ye. Nobody calls Eric McGrail a liar!"

Paddy called back as they negotiated the single-board steps, "No one's callin' ye a liar, mate, I was only sayin' that my Miggy ain't keepin' a rat down here."

The curtain had been ripped down from Miggy's alcove. Her navy blanket and few pitiful belongings were strewn about the cellar floor. However, there was no sign of Sailor. Eric shuffled about, squinching his face and holding on to his griping stomach. He kicked the tin of drinking water over and ground his boot down on on the bacon rind, eggshell and bread crusts.

"Tell the truth, girl, you've been keepin' a rat down here!"

Miggy shook her head. "No, I haven't, I don't like rats."

Eric glared at her from under beetling brows. "Don't take me for a fool, ye liddle liar!"

Atty interrupted his tirade. "Miggy good girl, not tell lies, she never keep rat!"

Eric turned on him furiously. "Then it's you, poisonin' me grub, ye son o' Satan!"

The Siamese cook folded his arms, gazing implacably at Eric. "If I want to poison you, long time ago you'd be dead. You make plenty foolish talk."

Completely lost for words, Eric pushed the cook aside and lurched over to the stairs. Then he turned, fixing the three of them with a malicious sneer. "So be it then. I'll cook me own grub from now on. But I warn ye, I'll get to the bottom o' the rat business. When I'm fit again, I'll send for Tommy Dyer, the rat catcher. Hah, no rat ever escapes Tommy, he'll catch the vermin alive an' sell it to the sportin' gang at the Slaughterhouse pub. They'll sling it in the pit with two rattin' terriers, then bet on which one'll tear your rat to bits first!"

When the trapdoor slammed shut, Miggy searched the cellar, calling out in a loud whisper, "Sailor, where are you, Sailor?" She gave a squeak of surprise when the mongoose dropped lightly onto her shoulders from out of the ceiling crossbeams. He licked Miggy's ear and curled about her neck. Paddy looked worried.

"I should've known it was wrong, bringin' a mongoose to Eric's place. I think I'd best take him back aboard ship."

Large tears popped from Miggy's eyes as she pleaded with her dad. "Oh, please don't take Sailor away from me, I love him so much! I'll hide him better this time, Uncle Eric will never know he's here. Let me keep him, please, Dad!"

Paddy McGrail had never seen his daughter cry since she was a babe in arms—it upset him. She was usually a tough little soul. He looked to the cook for help. "What d'you think, Atty, would it work out if I left him here?"

Atty Lok had quite firm views on the subject. "Paddy can no give daughter gift, then take away, not honourable! Leave Sailor here with Miggy, she take care of him. I look out for Eric, things be fine again."

Paddy relented. "Alright, Sailor stays. But Miggy, me darlin', don't let Eric see him, whatever ye do!"

At floodtide on the following morn, Paddy McGrail boarded the *Bengal Pearl* and sailed for Greenock. Miggy stood on the quay, waving, as the ship glided by under sail, like a huge white swan.

"Have a safe trip, Dad, see you next week. Don't worry, you-know-who will never catch sight of you-know-what!" She ran to the river wall, waving until the big clipper became a white smudge far up the River Mersey.

Miggy Mags continued her daily drudge at the Mersey Star Boardinghouse and Chandlery. Scrubbing floors, washing pots and dishes, serving food, plus a hundred and one other chores between dawn and dusk.

She was forced to take extra care, as her uncle's illness had not improved. Eric McGrail had not set foot outside in days, sitting in the corner of the dining room, full of self-pity. His expressions alternated between abject misery and rank foul temper. Miggy and Atty were run ragged keeping up with his orders and demands.

Whenever the girl got a chance, she would creep downstairs to look after Sailor. The cook had provided some things to keep the mongoose amused: an oval white pebble, which resembled an egg, and a small coil of cotton rope, which Sailor treated like a snake. Miggy liked watching her pet wrestle with the stone one moment, then pounce on the rope suddenly. She petted the little creature, feeding him Demerara sugar and some of Atty's rice cake. Sailor nuzzled her hand, then rummaged in her apron pocket, searching for more. Miggy whispered, "All gone, mate, all gone. Be a good boy an' I'll bring you somethin' nice for dinner tonight. Go an' play now, I've got work to do upstairs."

Eric was thumping his boot on the floor, and calling for her. "Girl! Where in the name o' blazes has that idle scut got to?"

When Miggy appeared, Eric pressed four pennies into her hand. "Go to the Maid of Erin. Ask Aggie the barmaid for four penn 'orth of dark Jamaica rum. Shift y'self, girl, an' don't dare spill any, d'ye hear?"

Miggy bobbed a curtsy. "Yes, Uncle Eric."

Atty, carrying a pail of rubbish out, escorted Miggy to the door, calling out scornfully, "Hah, four penny of Jamaicy rum, only fool drink that for sick belly. That rum burn holes in man's gut. Here, I give you two more pennies, get six pennies of Jamaicy rum, finish Eric off proper, for good!"

The girl trotted off up the cobbled avenue with Eric's voice echoing in her ears as he bellowed at the cook, "You mind your own business, ye heathen poisoner! If I want Jamaica rum, I'll have it. I know what's best fer me!"

Down in the cellar, Sailor had tired of his playthings. Scampering up into his perch among the ceiling beams, he amused himself by gnawing at the wooden planking overhead. Sniffing the kitchen odours of frying food and molasses from above, Sailor began ripping earnestly into the wood, thinking there might be eggs up there—his favourite food. The little creature's teeth and claws went furiously to work. He was determined to assess the egg situation of the Mersey Star's kitchen. Within half an hour, Sailor could see daylight showing through the pine boarding. He redoubled his efforts cheerfully.

A thick fog fell over the waterfront that evening, enveloping the Liverpool coast in a pall of impenetrable mist. The dining room was empty save for Eric, still

ensconced in his corner chair. With a jug of hot water
and a bottle containing the dregs of his rum, the boardinghouse keeper sprawled ungracefully, his chin resting on his chest, snoring aloud. Atty and Miggy had
crept off, down to the cellar, to feed Sailor. There was
not much for him—a few crusts, spread with lard,
dipped in sugar. The mongoose stayed up in the
rafters, busy at his work. Atty had tried climbing up
to coax Sailor down.

But the mongoose would have none of it. Miggy
stared up into the dark shadows, brushing away at the
splinters which drifted down on her. "Sailor, come
down here this instant! Be a good boy and come down,
there's nice supper for you. Come on, Sailor!"

The mongoose ignored her for once. It was Atty
who came scrambling down, brushing wood splinters
from his hair. "No can get near Sailor, him little
naughty beast, nearly bite Atty's finger again. Not listen to you, Miggs."

Stretching on tiptoe, the girl peered up into the
rafters. "But what's he doing up there? Sailor, Sailor,
come dow—"

Her voice was drowned out by an almighty bang—
the snapping of wood—and Eric McGrail bellowing
like a wounded buffalo.

Sailor had completed his task. He had burrowed
through the ceiling, up into the dining room. The
problem was that he had been digging directly alongside the leg of Eric's chair. With the weight of the big

fat man, the damaged floor broke. One of the chair legs broke through the weakened timber.

Sailor shot through the gap just in time as Eric fell awkwardly sideways, the furniture collapsing beneath him. Kicking and howling, he lay on the floor, trying to extricate himself from the wreckage of the chair. Sailor nimbly dodged the thrashing legs. He skipped up Eric's body, over the swollen stomach, across the chest, hopping across the horrified man's face. Miggy and Atty came rushing upstairs. Eric's voice rose to a panicked screech.

"Eeeeeyaaaah! The big rat! Ooooowaaaahhh, 'elp!"

Disturbed by the noise, Sailor went shooting round the room like a furred rocket. The girl and the cook had Eric half on his feet when he knocked them roughly aside and thudded off after the mongoose.

He chased Sailor round the dining room, aiming kicks and curses at him. Miggy screamed, "Leave Sailor alone! Don't hurt him, Uncle Eric, please!"

Upsetting chairs and tables, Eric pounded on, his face the colour of a beetroot. Sailor skipped nimbly ahead of him, always just out of reach. Miggy, seeing the mongoose coming her way, held out her arms to it. "Here, Sailor, come on, boy!"

He leaped into her arms. Holding her pet close, Miggy ran to the door, grappled with the latch, then sped free, out into the fog. Eric booted a table aside and went after her. Like a flash, Atty Lok was blocking the doorway in front of him.

"Leave girl alone, beast not rat, only mongoose, not harm you!"

Eric charged him, flooring the smaller man with windmilling fists and hefty boot kicks. He stepped over the cook's crumpled form, snarling at him, "I'm goin' to kill that rat, then I'm goin' to give that brat the beltin' she deserves, before I drag 'er off to the parish work'ouse. An' you, huh, you're finished round my place. Pack yer bags, an' be gone afore I gets back!"

Miggy was not sure which way to run, the fog was so dense out on the quayside. Clutching Sailor to her, she hurried about in the cocooning whiteness. Completely lost, the girl ran straight into an iron bollard. A yelp of pain escaped her lips as she staggered to one side, holding her bleeding kneecap. Miggy fell right into her uncle Eric's bulging stomach. He was standing with his belt off, holding up his trousers with one hand.

His face was livid with rage as he swung the broad, brass-buckled belt at her. "Gimme that dirty rat, or I'll skin the hide off yer!"

Miggy crouched and covered her head with one arm, protecting Sailor with her body, crying out as the belt struck her.

The force of the blow knocked Miggy off balance. The mongoose jumped from the girl's shoulders just as Miggy fell backward, hitting her head on the cobbles. The last thing she saw before she blacked out was her uncle Eric. He was gurgling horribly, grabbing at the mongoose, which had him tight by the throat.

Atty Lok heard the splash and limped forward, his bacon knife in one hand, the other holding down a swelling on his forehead. Ice-cold dock water sprayed into his face, causing him to stop right on the edge of the quay. The Siamese cook peered dazedly about him. He saw Miggy lying on the damp cobbles to his left. There was no sign of Eric McGrail, nor the mongoose.

A tall, gaunt man wearing a battered top hat and carrying a sack over one shoulder materialised through the swathes of fog. He saw Atty trying to pick Miggy up, and went to help. "What's been goin' on round 'ere? I'm Tommy Dyer, the rat catcher. Where's big Eric from the boardin'ouse? I've got business t'do with him."

Atty nodded urgently toward the Mersey Star. "Help me get girl inside, I tell you all about it."

Three minutes later, Tommy Dyer was at the top of the avenue, shouting around the Dock Road, "Man in the dock! Man in the dock! Help, help!"

In a short time, several folk emerged from the fog. One of them, a constable, took charge of the situation. "Right, someone get ropes and hooks, lanterns, too. Quick as you can. Now, sir, where did the man fall in? Take us there. You stop here, sonny, show the men with the ropes which way we've gone. Move sharp now, the tide's on the ebb!"

Miggy lay on the dining room counter. Atty was dabbing her knee with a solution of salt stirred into boiled water. She tried to rise, but he pushed her back,

whispering instructions. "You not speak, hear nothing, see nothing. If anyone ask you, stay quiet, Miggs,
let Atty do all talkin'."

It was quite a while before anyone came into the
boardinghouse. Sounds of ropes and grappling hooks
splashing could be heard amid the shouts from the
quay as the constable entered. He was accompanied by
Tommy Dyer, two Lock Gate Keepers, an overweight
washerwoman, and a well-dressed old gentleman with
a carriage driver attending him. Miggy closed her eyes,
feigning unconsciousness. She listened to what was
going on. The constable spoke first.

"No sign or trace of a body out there, did either of
you witness what happened?"

The well-dressed gentleman nodded politely to
Atty. "This chap may know something. I hardly think
the little girl would, though. She's completely unconscious."

Miggy felt like a baby as the washerwoman picked
her up. "Pore liddle thing! I'll make 'er a nice cuppa
tea, with lots of sugar in it. Come on, queen, let's get
ye in a comfy armchair wid a warm shawl about yeh.
Is there any vinegar an' a clean towel round 'ere? This
child's got a nasty lump, an' a bruise on the back of 'er
skull."

Miggy allowed herself to be treated by the kindly
washerwoman as she listened to Atty Lok's explanation. The Siamese cook sounded very believable. "I
see all, everythin', sir. Big rat, more bigger'n cat, he

come up through hole in floor over there, see. Girl scream an' run out onto quay, rat run out, too. But rat not chasin' girl, he runnin' away from me, I chase rat with big knife. I trip, fall down steps outside. Owner, Eric 'Grail, very brave feller, he run after big rat. Girl Miggs, she hit bollard, knock herself out in fog. I jump up, come runnin'. See Eric on edge of dock, he kick out at rat, slip. Eric fall on rat, both go over edge into water. Very sad, oh, yes. Eric fine feller, tryin' to save girl from rat. Cobbles wet, very slippy out there in fog, not see where water is. Girl hurt, man help me bring her in here. Very sad, sir!"

The constable took it down laboriously in his notebook. Everyone stayed silent until he had finished. He looked to Tommy Dyer. "Did you see any of this, girl being knocked senseless, man and big rat both falling into the dock?"

Tommy had found the dregs in the rum bottle, so he downed them. Puffing out his narrow chest importantly, he gave what he considered was his expert opinion. "Me name's Thomas Bernard Dyer. I'm h'employed by the Dock Board as h'official rodent controller. Ho, yes, h'officer, I've seen many a great big rat down 'ere, an' dealt with 'em, too, filfy vermints. I can show ye the scars if'n ye like?"

The well-dressed old gentleman interrupted. "I'm certain the constable has better things to do than inspecting your battle wounds. Speak straight, man, did you actually witness the incident?"

The rat catcher tugged his hat brim respectfully. "No, sir, I h'arrived too late. But I knows me rats, sir. If the h'Oriental chap says that's wot 'appened, then I'll back 'im h'all the way. Pore Eric McGrail got word to me only a few days back, askin' me to come round an' h'investigate a large vermint, said it was h'infestin' the premises. Huh, wish I'd a-come sooner. They pays me a 'andsome fee for big rats at the University Medical School. Life's cruel, ain't it, now I'm out o' pocket by two shillin's, an' big Eric's dead!"

The well-dressed gent took a coin from his waistcoat pocket and pressed it into Dyer's grimy palm. "No doubt you did your duty as you saw it. I don't think the constable need detain you further, thank you."

Tommy Dyer took the hint and departed, tugging at his hat.

Miggy, taken upstairs by the washerwoman, was installed in her uncle Eric's huge bed. It was so very comfortable, the stressful evening's events soon took their toll. She fell quickly into a deep sleep. Downstairs, the policeman had Atty sign his statement of testimony. Further people arrived—more police and two Waterguards in a rowboat with dragging equipment. The search of the dock waters continued throughout the night.

It was nine o'clock of the following morn when the search for Eric McGrail was abandoned. Miggy was sitting up in bed, where Atty was serving her a fine breakfast he had cooked specially. The constable tapped on the door and entered. He removed his helmet and shuffled awkwardly. "No sign of your uncle Eric, I'm afraid, miss. They think he must have been swept out into the river, what with the lock gates being open and the strong undercurrent. The Mersey can be a treacherous river, so the Waterguards tell me. Your uncle was a brave man, miss, I'm sorry."

As the policeman left the room, Miggy called out, "Did they find the big rat, Officer?"

He shook his head at her, and went downstairs, muttering, "Did they find the rat! Huh, kids these days, what'll they think of next, I wonder?"

Miggy buried her face in the pillow and wept bitterly. The cook patted her shoulder gently. "Not worry about Eric anymore, Miggs, he gone for good. Always remember Sailor, though, he was brave mongoose, he save you from Eric. Sailor was true friend, just like I say."

The *Bengal Pearl* returned to Liverpool in due course. She was soon cargoed up in record time and set sail once again, outward bound for India. However, the ship sailed minus Paddy McGrail, who had to stay home with his daughter and attend to family business.

The well-dressed older gentleman was a barrister. He had left his card with Atty. Paddy contacted him.

There was much coming and going between the Mersey Star and his offices during the next fortnight. The old gentleman's name was Mr. Dalzell Rice. He assured Paddy that he would expedite matters on his behalf. Miggy was puzzled by it all, but she never pestered her dad, who seemed as bewildered as herself.

One month later, a Coroner's Court was convened. Atty was required to attend, along with Miggy and her dad. Mr. Dalzell Rice was already there on their arrival. The coroner's verdict was that after the required period deemed by law, and in the light of evidence, Eric McGrail was declared officially missing, presumably dead by misadventure, his body having been swept out to sea.

They emerged into the sunlight, where Mr. Dalzell Rice showed them to his waiting carriage. He took them to his offices, which he referred to as "Chambers." Miggy and Atty were given cups of aromatic coffee and some dainty chocolate-covered biscuits. The office clerk raised his eyebrows on seeing Miggy taking coffee with her little finger extended. Atty wrinkled his nose playfully at her.

"Miggs look like very fine lady now, much growed up. You be eleventeen twenty-two next birthday, I think!"

The girl frowned over the rim of her cup at him. "Kindly drink your coffee, my good man!"

Paddy smiled as he signed his name to what looked like sheafs of official-looking papers. When the business was done, everybody shook hands. Miggy had never seen her dad looking so happy, his face a picture of joy.

Mr. Dalzell Rice gave them the use of his carriage and driver to get back home. They arrived at the Mersey Star Boardinghouse and Chandlery in time for lunch. Paddy McGrail leaped from the carriage and swept his daughter up in both arms.

"Well, Miggy, me darlin', welcome home! As the only survivin' relatives an' kin of the late Eric Mc-Grail, this all belongs to me an' you now, lock, stock an' barrel! No more sailin' for me. We're proprietors, me love, boardin'house owners. D'ye know what? I think the first thing I'm goin' to do is to double Atty's wages an' declare him dinin' room manager. Atty Lok, what d'ye think of that? Huh, where's that feller gone?"

Miggy, sitting on the doorstep, gestured inside. "Prob'ly making lunch for us."

Paddy looked down at the girl, who was dabbing her eyes on her sleeve and sniffing quietly. Full of concern, he sat down beside her. "Miggy, girl, what's the matter, darlin'?"

She blinked rapidly to dispel the tears and gazed out to sea. "It's Sailor. I miss him a lot, Dad. I wish he was here now. He was my friend, and I'll never see him again."

Paddy hugged her. "I know, darlin', I know. But you can't be sad forever, Miggs, cheer up. You'll soon be gettin' nice new clothes an' goin' to school . . . bet you'll make lots o' mates there. In the holidays we'll go out together to the beach, an' to the country, you, an' me, an' Atty, too!"

Miggy stood up slowly. "Won't be the same without Sailor, though."

As they entered the dining room, Miggy gasped. There was Atty, feeding an egg to Sailor. He grinned at them. "He waitin' here like old drownded cat. Shall I give him another egg? This mongoose look hungry. Where you been, eh?"

Miggy dashed to the counter with her arms held wide. "Sailor, oh, Sailor, you came back, you're alive!"

The mongoose leaped into her arms. He licked the girl's face, leaving traces of raw egg all over her cheeks.

Paddy McGrail could only shake his head in wonderment. "Well, can ye beat that, Sailor's finished goin' to sea, too!"

Miggy placed her pet on the counter. "Give him eleventy-seven eggs, Atty, he deserves them!"

Atty grinned. "I give him eleventy-eight if he tell me where he been. See, Miggs, I tell you, mongoose friend for life!"

Miggy nodded fervently. "I believe you, Atty, I always did!"

Rosie's Pet

GO LOCK YOUR DOORS EACH EVENING,
bar all the windows tight—
young Rosie and her boyfriend
are on the prowl tonight.
Don't snigger at my warning,
you'll hear as they pass through.
Your marrow will freeze to a cry on the
    breeze,
it sounds like this—
    Aaaawwwwwooooooooooooooooh!

In a fight, Rosie Glegg could knock spots off any boy in her age group. She never played with other girls, hated frocks, dresses, skirts and ribbons. Rosie used dolls as target practice for her catapult shooting; her skipping rope served well as a lasso. She was always lassoing boys—the pale, studious types fled in terror from her expertly aimed loop.

Rosie Glegg wore jeans and Doc Marten boots. She also kept her hair cut short. She was the proud owner of a Swiss Army knife, which came in handy for cutting up other little girls' skipping ropes. Rosie harassed the local Boy Scouts and Girl Guide clubs, drove her teachers to distraction and was the scourge of librarians, playing park attendants, shopkeepers, bus drivers, etc., etc.

In the small rural English village of Nether Cum Hopping, Rosie Glegg was infamous during the nineteen sixties. Which was not bad going, considering she was only eight years old and had been grounded more times than a wingless plane.

It was the summer holidays. All sensible villagers

had fled on vacation to the European Continent, making sure they were well out of Rosie's reach. Her poor father seldom ventured his family on such trips, fearing an international incident. He often suffered nightmares from something that occurred on a family jaunt to London. Mr. Glegg was still paying damages to the National Heritage Trust for the depredations his daughter had caused to the Tower of London. As a result, he had to work long overtime hours repaying the bank loan. The plus side of this was that Mr. Glegg did not have to come home until Rosie was safely installed in bed.

Mrs. Edith Glegg, Rosie's mother, was a wan-looking, long-suffering lady. Several times she had tried changing her name to Whegg, Flegg, Pegg and, even adopting a Scandinavian accent, calling herself Olegg. This did not fool the female populace, who would point her out on the High Street, whispering to one another, "Look, there's Rosie Glegg's mother, poor soul!"

One sunny afternoon, when the other children were off on distant holidays, Rosie was in a rare peaceful mood. She sat by the pond in the local woods, skimming flat stones across the water's surface. She looked so placid that one or two of the bolder frogs plucked up courage to watch her from the reeds on the far bank. That was when the boy appeared on the scene. He was about the same age as her, and equally scruffy. Rosie ignored him for a while, then, on a sudden impulse, selected a flat stone and gave it a super-skilful skim. It bounced off the water seven times. Rosie nodded at the young intruder.

"See that? I'm Rosie Glegg, the best stone skimmerer inna world. Betcha can't skim stones s'good as me!"

She tossed him a stone, a round bumpy one, which she knew would be useless to skim with. He tried it. Like all bumpy round stones, it vanished with a single plop. They watched the ripples spread over the pond. Rosie scoffed.

"Yahaa! See, I told ya. What's y'name?"

Throwing himself on the grassy bank, the boy rolled over and shook himself, like a dog. He had a grin like a slice of red watermelon with a lollopy tongue. "Charlie Lupus."

Rosie tried to keep her face straight as he grinned at her. Absently he scratched his stomach with a bare foot. She was so taken by his infectious grin that she did not even bother reaching for the skipping rope lasso. "Charlie Lupus, eh, great name. What d'you do, Charlie?"

Giggling hoarsely, he produced a piece of stick and gave it to her. "Just you throw that!"

Rosie tested the stick's balance. "Where d'you want me to sling it?"

Charlie shrugged. "Anywhere. Go on, chuck it hard!"

Leaping to her feet, Rosie whirled and flung the

stick, high and hard. Up and out it went, off into the tangled woodlands. Rosie blinked in surprise as Charlie took off like a bullet. She marvelled at his speed, and how he disregarded for bush and bramble, merely leaping over them or crashing right through.

Before she had time to think, Charlie Lupus was back, with the stick held in his mouth. He dropped it at Rosie's feet and lay on his back, cheerfully grinning and panting, his tongue lolloping out to one side. She was impressed.

"Triffick, but why d'you carry the stick in y'mouth?"

"Dunno, s'easier, I s'pose."

"Zoweee! Y'must be the best stick fetcherer inna world, betcha you're better'n a dog even!"

The odd boy shook matted hair from his eyes. "Yeah, I'm better'n any ole dog!"

"Whereja live?"

"Anywhere, here mostly."

Rosie shook her head, laughing. "Haha, I think you're crackers, Charlie Lupus!"

His wild, dark eyes challenged her. "Crackers yourself, Rosie Glegg! Anyhow, what can you do 'sides skimmin' stones 'cross the water?"

Rosie picked up her skipping rope. "Lasso boys."

Charlie began dodging and stooping. "Go on then, betcha can't lasso me!"

She shook out the noose, twirling it lazily, watching him ducking and weaving. Choosing the right moment, Rosie flicked the rope at him. It was not an ideal cast. Instead of pinning his arms to his sides, the noose settled around Charlie's neck. He stood still, mischief sparkling from his eyes. "Good throw, Rosie, come on, let's go for a run."

He took off like lightning, towing her behind as he tore madly around the lake bank. Rosie galloped after him, the rope wrapped around her wrist. She was pulled frantically along, unable to stop the headlong dash. Twice round the lake they sped, then Rosie stumbled and tripped. Charlie flopped down beside her, panting and chuckling. Rosie stared at him, wide-eyed.

"Nuts, that's what you are, y'could've been choked by that rope."

Charlie pulled the tightened noose from his neck. He laughed scornfully. "Can't choke me, my neck's too strong!"

Kneeling on all fours at the lake edge, he began thirstily lapping up water. Rosie laughed uproariously at his antics. "Yaaahahahaha! Toldya you're bonkers. What's it taste like?"

Charlie licked his lips. "Smashin', come'n'try some."

A gamekeeper watched the scene unfold from his hideout in the bushes. Two lads—no, wait, it was a boy and girl. Children, crouching like animals, lapping up lake water. Disgusting! He strode officiously forward, shotgun tucked beneath his arm, to confront them. "Stop that, you filthy little beasts. Stop this instant!"

Rosie turned to stare at him. Charlie just sniffed and continued slurping up water. The keeper nudged him with the toe of his boot.

"You, boy, are you deaf?"

Charlie wiped the back of his hand across his chin. "Course I'm not deaf. I could hear you comin' ages before you got here."

Resting the gun loosely in the crook of his arm, the gamekeeper gave them his officially stern gaze. "You're both trespassing on private land, you shouldn't be anywhere near these woods. What's your name, little girl?"

Rosie smiled innocently. "Little girl."

He pointed at her warningly. "Don't be so impudent. I know you, you're the Glegg kid. Huh, born troublemaker. Now, where d'you live, young man?"

Charlie spread both arms in a carefree gesture. "Here."

The gamekeeper decided that he had put up with enough insolence. He took hold of their arms, squeezing slightly, to let them know he meant business. "Now clear off, the pair of you. If I catch you ag— Yowch!"

Charlie Lupus's teeth nipped the man's hand. In the same movement he grabbed Rosie's wrist and sped off. She gasped for breath as he whirled her along. Trees and bushes humming past her in a green blur, Rosie's feet pounded the earth, fifty to the dozen. She was dragged madly onward, with Charlie's wild laughter ringing in her ears. They charged headlong, crashing through brambles, leaping ditches, bounding through leafy glades. Behind them, the keeper's angry cries faded into the high sunny afternoon.

Emerging from the woodlands, Rosie steered Charlie over to the bus terminal. She pointed out great horse chestnut trees, boasting that only she could climb them. Charlie Lupus shook his head, dappled sunlight playing on his tawny mop.

"Don't like climbin', I'm best at runnin'!"

There were big houses with driveways on the opposite side of the lane. A huge German shepherd dog came pelting out of the first one. Snarling viciously, fangs bared and back bristling, it came at them. Rosie Glegg was not afraid of dogs. She cast about for a stone to throw at it. Charlie suddenly dropped on all fours, showing his teeth. He gave voice to a weird, blood-curdling howl, and ran at the dog.

The transformation was immediate. With a pitiful yelp, the big dog turned. It fled back up the driveway, whining, its tail curled between its back legs. Rosie stared at him in admiration. "Good ole Charlie, how'd you do that?"

Wrinkling his nose, her friend gave a funny little growl. "S'easy, I'll teach you sometime. Hey, watch this, Rosie!"

A tabby cat with half-closed eyes was squatting on

top of an ornamental gatepost, paying scant attention to them. Charlie narrowed his lips and faced the cat. He gave a short, fierce bark. The cat leapt from the gatepost into a nearby beech tree. Clawing its way swiftly into the thin upper branches, it swayed there, meowing pleadingly for help.

Rosie patted her friend's back. "That'll be good practice for the firemen, they like rescuin' cats."

Charlie lolloped up the lane ahead of her. He knew he needed to get Rosie out of the park. "C'mon, there's a bus just ready to leave."

The bus driver looked on despairingly as the ragged moppet boarded his vehicle. He had spent many perilous journeys ferrying Rosie Glegg around the area. Cursing his ill luck silently, he accepted the well-chewed return ticket and started the engine. Rosie was the sole passenger as the bus rumbled off. Charlie ran easily beside the vehicle with a steady lope. He called to Rosie as she clambered over the seats, opening all the windows wide.

"See you tomorrow, I'll be by the lake!"

Rosie hung halfway out of the last window. "What about tonight? I'll escape from home, where'll you be?"

Charlie halted in a cloud of dust as the bus accelerated. "Maybe in the adventure playground. . . . Maybe!"

Rosie Glegg knelt on the backseat, waving, as her strange new pal diminished into the distance. She smiled, a rare and beautiful smile, imagining the fun they could have together. Then she turned and began pulling hideous faces, which the driver could see in his rearview mirror. Cramming a fistful of antistress tablets into his mouth, the object of her attention drove heedlessly through a red light, anxious to reach 152 Trafalgar Crescent, the Glegg residence.

Rosie retired to her bedroom promptly at eight-thirty every evening. Her careworn mother collapsed in an easy chair, knowing that on the dot of eight forty-five, her husband would arrive home. Mr. Glegg would tiptoe in, fervently hoping that his daughter would be asleep. Some hope! At nine o'clock Rosie shimmied nimbly down the back drainpipe, leapt onto the toolshed roof and scrambled over the rear fence to commence her night ramble.

Back at the house, Mrs. Glegg wearily collected a blackened towel from the bathroom. She removed Rosie's two pet spiders (Ivan and Ignatius) from the bath. After replacing the soap (with the initials *R.G.* carved into it) to the soap holder, she tiptoed wearily downstairs, passing the bedroom door with the purple felt-tipped warning.

KEEP OWT + BEEWHERR OV KROKKERDIALS. YOOVBEEN WHORNED BUY ROWZEE G.

Mrs. Glegg kept out, knowing by some of the noises which emanated from Rosie's bedroom the presence of crocodiles could not be ruled out. In the living room, she showed Mr. Glegg the latest letter from their eldest son, Dennis. He had gone to work among the headhunters of the Orotwango Basin in darkest Amazoniga. Her husband sighed wistfully as he scanned his son's epistle.

"Trust Dennis to choose the soft life and leave us here with Rosie!"

There was no sign of Charlie Lupus at the adventure playground. Rosie sat twirling the high security padlock, which she had opened with her Swiss Army knife. As dusk was starting to fall, she had done what she could with the playground apparatus. All the swing and climbing ropes she had knotted together with secret sailor knots, which were impossible to untie. Rosie had shifted most of the sandpit into the paddling pool, where she constructed a dam. There was not much else to do but wait now.

She chided herself for not making Charlie take the Slimy Green Death Oath that he would turn up.

The night crept on, with a beautiful apricot-hued full moon appearing to illuminate the darkness. Rosie was starting to lose patience. At first she did not see the massive grey dog lurking nearby. It sat watching her from the cover of a heavy-timbered climbing frame, its brown-amber flecked eyes glowing like twin flames.

Then the dog approached. Padding around the back of her, silent as a cloud shadow, it leaned over the nape of her exposed neck. Rosie's flesh gleamed grimy white in the moonlight. Licking its slavering lips, the dog opened its mouth hungrily, exposing dangerous ivory-hued canine fangs. They drew closer to the girl's unprotected neck. . . . Closer! Then it gave her a huge, slurping, playful lick.

"Yurrk! Gerroff!"

Rosie was aware of the perils of neck washing, whether by soap, flannel or dog tongue. All could prove fatal in her estimation. As the dog attempted a second lick, she shoved it away. "Gerroff me, y'silly pooch, go 'way an' play!"

She found a stick and threw it, hoping the beast would leave her in peace. In an instant, the dog was back with the stick. Laying it at her feet, it sat beside Rosie, lolloping and panting. It reminded her of her friend. "I know, I'll call you Charlie, d'you like that?"

"Woof!"

"D'you know ole Charlie? You look awful like him."

"Woof woof!"

"Good feller, d'you know where he is?"

The big dog threw back its head and bayed. *"Yaaaawwooooohhh!"*

Rosie Glegg felt the hair on her head rise up straight, an electric tingle coursing up and down her spine. The howl of the grey dog was more exciting than anything she had ever experienced in her short, but full, life. Visions swirled behind its moonlit eyes, strange sights of snowbound forests, craggy mountains and far-off ruined castles.

Rosie heard the cries of frightened peasants rising above the smoke of flaring torchlights. A wild urgency tugging at her nerve ends, she looped her skipping rope around the huge beast's thickly furred neck.

"Come on, Charlie, let's go to the woods!"

Both dog and girl burst from the adventure playground, baying aloud their homage to the watching moon. *"Aaaaaaaoooooooowwwwwoooooooh!"*

The good villagers of Nether Cum Hopping shuddered as eerie howls echoed about their streets. Children tugged bedsheets over their heads and trembled. Curtains were hastily drawn, doors slammed and tightly bolted. Lights flicked on, setting houses ablaze with illumination for protection against the chilling sounds. Confusion reigned. Telephones jangled, jamming up the switchboards with calls to the police and the Noise Abatement Society (only recorded messages after five P.M.). The R.S.P.C.A. (Royal Society for Prevention of Cruelty to Animals) sent out a two-man patrol, looking for two dogs which somebody had roped together—or was it a child and a dog? The officers were set upon by a large German shepherd dog which lived in the lane alongside the woods. After fending it off, they reported the incident to the police, who took out a warrant against its owner. The police, however, were not convinced that it was any type of animal noise. They closed down a disco, confiscated a boom box from a group of teenagers on a street corner and issued a ticket to a young man driving a sports car (whose horn played four consecutive tunes, starting with "La Cucaracha" and culminating in "Colonel Bogey"). The Noise Abatement Society remained silent throughout the entire operation.

The Directors of Greenacres Investments P.L.C. slept soundly many miles away in London. G.I.P.L.C., as they were known, had recently purchased the woods from the Urban District Council with a view to developing it as a sporting area for upwardly mobile shooting clubs and rich foreign tourists (on the agreement that the adjacent public fields be converted into a private car park). Of late, Greenacres had been concerned with the dwindling numbers of pheasants, woodgrouse, woodpigeons, woodcock, partridge and quail. They prepared a report for their shareholders, stating that the area would be patrolled, night and day, by two gamekeepers. These men would guard the living assets (gamebirdwise), protecting them until such time as the paid members were ready to blast the birds with their custom-made shotguns. Also, they would discourage any local activities (poachingwise), thereby rendering said woodland tract a viable investment (shootingwise), whilst still complying with parliamentary regulations (environmentwise).

Clouds drifted serenely across the apricot moon, as trees and bushes swayed in the soft breeze, causing shadowy patterns through the nightshaded woodland.

Rosie Glegg felt the warm rush of air as she was hauled swiftly along by the big grey dog. Its keen eyes were everywhere at once as it weaved twixt oak and elm, slid around juniper and laurel, and bounded over thistle and gorse, never once stumbling on protruding root or rock. Rosie's wild young soul was filled to overflowing with exhilaration. She sniffed hungrily at newfound aromas. Pheasant, which smelled better than hamburger, partridge that no hot dog sausage could equal. Oh, why had she been born a mere human, forced to wear clothes and shoes instead of having fur and paws? Why could she not be a dog? Better one night as Rover than a lifetime as Rosie!

Her dog, Charlie, halted, his body quivering with anticipation. Rosie sensed it, too. Danger and adventure combined. Together they crouched in a fern bed, watching the unsuspecting gamekeeper's back.

Gamekeeper Gordon M. Liggett perched upon his folding campstool, nibbling at a cucumber-and-marmalade sandwich. Nearby, his double-barrelled shotgun lay loaded and close to hand. Approximately six yards from where he sat in hiding, a cock and hen pheasant stood tethered to a slender rowan trunk. Gordon M. sipped Lapsang Oolong tea from his vacuum flask as he watched the live bait he had set up. Hah! Local poachers, he'd show 'em! Those working-class thieves always fell, hook, line and sinker, for the old brace of pheasant trick. He curled his lip scornfully at the unseen culprits as he pictured the scenario. Two village ne'er-do-wells clad in cheap, discount-store fashion. Probably full to the gills with beer and armed with catalogue-purchased Czechoslovakian air pistols. Hunting unlicensed for game birds, which they would doubtless sell to the Manor Restaurant and Carvery, thereby supplementing their generous State Unemployment Benefit. He imagined their conversation.

"Cor, stripe me pink, 'arry, a coupla peasants for the bag!"

"Haha, them's pheasants, Reg, we're peasants. Still, they'll do nicely, thank yew. Wait'll I get a bead on 'em!"

At this point, Gordon M. would step majestically from cover, shotgun at the ready. "Stand perfectly still, you two louts! I am a licensed gamekeeper for Greenacres P.L.C., and I'll stand no jiggery pokery from either of you felons. Drop those pistols, hand over that sack marked swag. Now, quick march to the police station. This gun has hair triggers, y'know!"

"Blimey, don't shoot, Guv, we've both got families!"

"We wasn't doin' nuffink, sir, just gavverin' wildflowers!"

"Tell it to the marines, laddie, the game's up for you two."

Gordon M. chuckled to himself. He was the very fellow for the job. Greenacres Investments P.L.C. would soon realise that they had hired a professional gamekeeper. Unlike that other oaf, Patterson, who had let himself get bitten by a couple of kids on the day shift. Huh, he'd let them escape, too!

A rustling from the ferns interrupted his meanderings. Gordon M. Liggett's hands began shaking—he realised that he was scared. Well, sitting out alone in these woods at night, there could be a whole gang of poachers stealing up on him. His confidence was restored when he saw the shotgun lying nearby. He reached for it. Suddenly a lot of things happened all at once.

As he touched the gun, something barged roughly into him, knocking him sideways. Falling from his folding campstool, he sat down squarely on his vacuum flask. It splintered, injuring his bottom with hot tea and tiny glass shards. Gordon M. gave an odd squeak of dismay, which mingled with the cackling of pheasants as they were seized by someone, or something. His gun missing, he struggled upright, treading upon his unwrapped sandwiches.

He saw a little girl standing in a patch of moonlight over by the lake. She was swinging his shotgun by the barrels. Before he could stop her, she flung it into the water. It vanished with a single splash. Gordon M. felt his fear replaced by wrath and indignation.

So that was their game. Bringing a little kid to steal his gun and distract his attention! He ran in the direction of the bushes where the child had gone.

"Halt! Stand still this instant, you're in very deep trouble, young lady!"

Despite the fact that he was running pell-mell, Gordon M. Liggett froze in his tracks at the sight which confronted him. It was a wolf!

A great, grey, long-legged, fiery-eyed, sharp-fanged wolf!

The little girl stood with one hand buried in the bristling collar fur of the brute's neck. Both the child and the beast snarled viciously, advancing stiff-legged toward him. Their snarls turned into a long, savage hunting cry.

"Aaaaaaawwwwwwoooooooh!"

Gordon M. Liggett's nerve deserted him miserably. A panicked gurgle escaped his lips. He turned and fled for his life. Cucumber sandwiches sticking to his feet and a damaged posterior did not hinder him. Truth to tell, they seemed to lend speed to his desperate dash. Away from the life of a gamekeeper, far from wild wolves, mad little girls and nightdark woods. Away to traffic fumes, noise, light and paved streets filled with the presence of people.

The moon had receded behind a cloudbank. Back in the woods, Rosie Glegg sat beside her wolf, whom she knew was her friend Charlie Lupus. His tongue lolled out as she removed pheasant feathers from his stiff grey whiskers. Rosie took his face in her hands.

"Can I be a wolf, too, Charlie? I'd make a good wolf. Please!"

They sat facing one another, blue eyes gazing into amber-streaked brown ones. The moon emerged from the cloud. Rosie saw it reflected twice in Charlie's wolf eyes, which watched her unblinkingly. Eyes within moons, moons within eyes. Running, baying, sniffing, knowing every secret path through the realms of night by their feel, by their smell, by their mysterious call. In a flash, Rosie was seeing more clearly than ever before, though everything was bathed in a pale, brownish-yellow light. She rubbed her eyes with her hand . . . or was it her paw?

Rosie Glegg gave a growling laugh. Charlie Lupus gave a laughing growl.

They drank their fill at the lake and roamed the woods all night, side by side.

Pink-cheeked, happy Mrs. Glegg hummed as she prepared dinner for her husband. These days he came home early so that he could see his little daughter, Rosie. Mrs. Glegg smiled joyfully. What a change in Rosie, even though she preferred her hamburgers and sausages raw. Things were vastly different since she had brought her new friend to the house. Charles Lupus, what a nice boy, so quiet, too. He could sleep in Dennis's old room for as long as he pleased. Rosie was a different character now, no more wanton acts of terrorism upon other little girls, no more fighting with boys. She had given up her Swiss Army knife and abandoned the fearsome skipping-rope lariat. Long, quiet walks with Charlie were the order of the day for

Rosie now, especially since the woodlands were once more open to the public. So sensible of Greenacres Investments P.L.C. to pull out of their proposed development. It said in the *Nether Cum Hopping Daily Euphonium* that the company had moved to Scotland. Nine hundred acres of moorland in Auchterfloogle. Greenacres could keep a full stock of gamebirds unscathed there, ready to be blown into oblivion by foreign tourists and overstressed executives.

Skipping blithely upstairs, Mrs. Glegg cooed softly, "Rosie, Charles, dinner's almost ready now!"

She hummed her way downstairs, not bothering either of them by entering their rooms. Children needed somewhere private to call their own. Even the notices on bedroom doors were not what they used to be. Evidently, crocodiles had fallen out of favour. The writing on both doors now probably owed much to the scaremongering of the local press. Mrs. Glegg surmised that they owed a lot to the printing errors of the papers, too.

KEEYP OWT. DAINJER! WHAIRWULFS LIV HEER. ROWZEE GEE AN CHARLEE EL.

Epilogue

Gordon M. Liggett became antisocial after the cost of a double-barrelled shotgun was deducted from his severance pay by his former employers, Greenacres Investments P.L.C. He was arrested by the police following a complaint from the Noise Abatement Society that he had been causing annoyance to customers in the bar parlour of the Railway Arms public house by continually howling like a wolf. A further charge of kicking a German shepherd dog outside of No 1 Woodside Lane was dismissed by the police. However, the Royal Society for the Prevention of Cruelty to Animals (R.S.P.C.A.) will be taking out a private summons for legal action against the said Gordon M. Liggett the moment he gets out of psychiatric counselling.